THE FAIRY
CARAVAN

Louisa Pussy-cat Sleeps Late

THE FAIRY
CARAVAN

THE ORIGINAL AND AUTHORIZED EDITION

BY BEATRIX POTTER™

F. WARNE & Co

FREDERICK WARNE

Published by the Penguin Group
27 Wrights Lane, London W8 5TZ, England
Penguin Books USA Inc., 375 Hudson Street, New York, New York 10014, USA
Penguin Books Australia Ltd, Ringwood, Victoria, Australia
Penguin Books Canada Ltd, 10 Alcorn Avenue, Toronto, Ontario, Canada M4V 3B2
Penguin Books (N.Z.) Ltd, 182-190 Wairau Road, Auckland 10, New Zealand

Penguin Books Ltd, Registered Offices: Harmondsworth, Middlesex, England

First published 1929
This edition with new reproductions of Beatrix Potter's illustrations
first published 1992 by Frederick Warne
3 5 7 9 10 8 6 4 2

ISBN 0 7232 4044 2

Printed and bound in Great Britain by
BPC Hazells Ltd

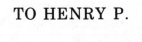

TO HENRY P.

Preface

As I walk'd by myself,
And talked to myself,
 Myself said unto me –

Through many changing seasons these tales have
walked and talked with me. They were not meant
for printing; I have left them in the homely idiom
of our old north country speech. I send them on the
insistence of friends beyond the sea.

Beatrix Potter

Contents

CHAPTER 1

Tuppenny

In the Land of Green Ginger there is a town called
Marmalade, which is inhabited exclusively by
guinea-pigs. They are of all colours, and of two
sorts. The common, or garden, guinea-pigs are the
most numerous. They have short hair, and they
run errands and twitter. The guinea-pigs of the
other variety are called Abyssinian Cavies. They
have long hair and side whiskers, and they walk
upon their toes. The common guinea-pigs admire
and envy the whiskers of the Abyssinian Cavies;
they would give anything to be able to make their
own short hair grow long. So there was excitement
and twittering amongst the short-haired guinea-
pigs when Messrs. Ratton and Scratch, Hair

Specialists, sent out hundreds of advertisements by post, describing their new elixir.

The Abyssinian Cavies who required no hair stimulant were affronted by the advertisements. They found the twitterings tiresome.

During the night between March 31st and April 1st, Messrs. Ratton and Scratch arrived in Marmalade. They placarded the walls of the town with posters; and they set up a booth in the market place. Next morning quantities of elegantly stoppered bottles were displayed upon the booth. The rats stood in front of the booth, and distributed handbills describing the wonderful effects of their new quintessence. 'Come buy, come buy, come buy! Buy a bottleful and try it on a door-knob! We guarantee that it will grow a crop of onions!' shouted Messrs. Ratton and Scratch. Crowds of short-haired guinea-pigs swarmed around the booth.

The Abyssinian Cavies sniffed, and passed by upon their toes. They remarked that Mr. Ratton was slightly bald. The short-haired guinea-pigs continued to crowd around, twittering and asking questions; but they hesitated to buy. The price of a very small bottle holding only two thimblefuls was ten peppercorns.

And besides this high charge there was an uncomfortable doubt as to what the stuff was made of. The Abyssinian Cavies spread ill-natured reports that it was manufactured from slugs. Mr.

'Come buy, come buy, come buy!'

Scratch emphatically contradicted this slander; he asserted that it was distilled from the purest Arabian moonshine; 'And Arabia is quite close to Abyssinia,' said Mr. Scratch with a wink, pointing to a particularly long-haired Abyssinian Cavy. 'Come buy a sample bottle, can't you! Listen to these testimonials from our grateful customers,' said Mr. Ratton. He proceeded to read aloud a number of letters. But he did not specifically deny a rumour that got about; about a certain notorious nobleman, a much married nobleman, who had bought a large bottle of the quintessence by persuasion of the first of his eight wives. This nobleman – so the story ran – had used the hair stimulant with remarkable results. He had grown a magnificent beard. But the beard was blue. Which may be fashionable in Arabia; but the short-haired guinea-pigs were dubious. Messrs. Ratton and Scratch shouted themselves hoarse. 'Come buy a sample bottle half price, and try it for salad dressing! The cucumbers will grow of themselves while you are mixing the hair oil and vinegar! Buy a sample bottle, can't you?' shouted Messrs. Ratton and Scratch. The short-haired guinea-pigs determined to purchase one bottle of the smallest size, to be tried upon Tuppenny.

Tuppenny was a short-haired guinea-pig of dilapidated appearance. He suffered from tooth-ache and chilblains; and he had never had much hair, not even of the shortest. It was thin and patchy. Whether this was the result of chilblains or of ill-treatment is uncertain. He was an object, whatever the cause. Obviously he was a suitable subject for experiment. 'His appearance can scarcely become worse, provided he does not turn blue,' said his friend Henry P.; 'let us subscribe for a small bottle, and apply it as directed.'

So Henry P. and nine other guinea-pigs bought a bottle and ran in a twittering crowd towards Tuppenny's house. On the way, they overtook Tuppenny going home. They explained to him that out of sympathy they had subscribed for a bottle of moonshine to cure his toothache and chilblains, and that they would rub it on for him as Mrs. Tuppenny was out.

Tuppenny was too depressed to argue; he allowed himself to be led away. Henry P. and the nine other guinea-pigs poured the whole bottleful over Tuppenny, and put him to bed. They wore gloves themselves while applying the quintess-ence. Tuppenny was quite willing to go to bed; he felt chilly and damp.

Presently Mrs. Tuppenny came in; she com-plained about the sheets. Henry P. and the other guinea-pigs went away. After tea they returned at 5.30. Mrs. Tuppenny said nothing had happened.

The short-haired guinea-pigs took a walk; they looked in again at 6. Mrs. Tuppenny was abusive. She said there was no change. At 6.30 they called again to inquire. Mrs. Tuppenny was still more

Tuppenny was too depressed to argue.

abusive. She said Tuppenny was very hot. Next time they came she said the patient was in a fever, and felt as if he were growing a tail. She slammed the door in their faces and said she would not open it again for anybody.

Henry P. and the other guinea-pigs were perturbed. They betook themselves to the market place, where Messrs. Ratton and Scratch were still trying to sell bottles by lamplight, and they asked anxiously whether there was any risk of tails growing? Mr. Scratch burst into ribald laughter; and Mr. Ratton said – 'No sort of tail except pigtails on the head!'

During the night Messrs. Ratton and Scratch packed up their booth and departed from the town of Marmalade.

Next morning at daybreak a crowd of guinea-pigs collected on Tuppenny's doorstep. More and more arrived until Mrs. Tuppenny came out with a scrubbing brush and a pail of water. In reply to inquiries from a respectful distance, she said that Tuppenny had had a disturbed night. Further she would not say, except that he was unable to keep on his nightcap. No more could be ascertained, until, providentially, Mrs. Tuppenny discovered

that she had nothing for breakfast. She went out to buy a carrot.

Henry P. and a crowd of other guinea-pigs swarmed into the house, as soon as she was round the corner of the street. They found Tuppenny out of bed, sitting on a chair, looking frightened. At least, presumably it was Tuppenny, but he looked different. His hair was over his ears and nose. And that was not all; for whilst they were talking to him, his hair grew down onto his empty plate. It grew something alarming. It was quite nice hair and the proper colour; but Tuppenny said he felt funny; sore all over, as if his hair were being brushed back to front; and prickly and hot, like needles and pins; and altogether uncomfortable.

And well he might! His hair – it grew, and it grew, and it grew; faster and faster and nobody knew how to stop it! Messrs. Ratton and Scratch had gone away and left no address. If they

16

Still the hair kept growing.

possessed an antidote there was no way of obtaining it. All day that day, and for several days – still the hair kept growing. Mrs. Tuppenny cut it, and cut it, and stuffed pin-cushions with it, and pillow cases and bolsters; but as fast as she cut it – it grew again. When Tuppenny went out he tumbled over it; and the rude little guinea-pig boys ran after him, shouting 'Old Whiskers!' His life became a burden.

Then Mrs. Tuppenny began to pull it out. The effect of the quintessence was beginning to wear off, if only she would have exercised a little patience; but she was tired of cutting; so she pulled. She pulled so painfully and shamelessly that Tuppenny could not stand it. He determined to run away – away from the hair pulling and the chilblains and the long-haired and the short-haired guinea-pigs, away and away, so far away that he would never come back.

So that is how it happened that Tuppenny left his home in the town of Marmalade, and wandered into the world alone.

CHAPTER 2

The Travelling Circus

In after years Tuppenny never had any clear recollection of his adventures while he was running away. It was like a bad mixed up dream that changes into morning sunshine and is forgotten. A long, long journey: noisy, jolting, terrifying; too frightened and helpless to understand anything that happened before the journey's end. The first thing that he remembered was a country lane, a steep winding lane always climbing up hill. Tuppenny ran and ran, splashing through the puddles with little bare feet. The wind blew cold against him; he wrapped his hands in his mop of hair, glad to feel its pleasant warmth over his ears and nose. It had stopped growing, and his chilblains had disappeared. Tuppenny felt like a new guinea-pig. For the first time he smelt the air of the hills. What matter if the wind were chilly; it blew from the mountains. The lane led to a wide common, with hillocks and hollows and clumps of bushes. The short cropped turf would soon be gay with wild flowers; even in early April it was sweet. Tuppenny felt as though he could run for miles. But night was coming. The sun was going down in a frosty orange sunset behind purple clouds – was it clouds, or was it the hills? He looked for shelter, and saw smoke rising behind some tall savin bushes.

Tuppenny advanced cautiously, and discovered a curious little encampment. There were two vehicles, unharnessed; a small shaggy pony was grazing nearby. One was a two-wheeled cart, with a tilt, or hood, made of canvas stretched over hoops. The other was a tiny four-wheeled caravan. It was painted yellow picked out with red. Upon the sides were these words in capital letters – 'ALEXANDER AND WILLIAM'S CIRCUS.' Upon another board was printed – The Pigmy Elephant! The Learned Pig! The Fat Dormouse of Salisbury! Live Polecats and Weasels!

The caravan had windows with muslin curtains, just like a house. There were outside steps up to the back door, and a chimney on the roof. A canvas screen fastened to light posts sheltered the encampment from the wind. The smoke which Tuppenny had seen did not come from the chimney; there was a cheerful fire of sticks burning on the ground in the midst of the camp.

Several animals sat beside it, or busied themselves with cooking. One of them was a white West Highland terrier. When he noticed Tuppenny he commenced to bark. The pony stopped grazing, and looked round. A bird, who had been running up and down on the grass, flew up to the roof of the caravan.

The little dog came forward barking. Tuppenny turned and fled. He heard yap! yap! yap! and grunt, grunt, grunt! and pattering feet behind him. He tripped over his hair, and fell in a twittering heap.

A cold nose and a warm tongue examined Tuppenny and turned him over. He gazed up in terror at the little dog and a small black pig, who were sniffing all over him. 'What? what? what? Whatever sort of animal is it, Sandy?' 'Never saw the like! it seems to be all hair! What do you call yourself, fuzzy wig?' 'P-p-please sir, I'm not a fuzzy wig, a fuzzy pig, a please sir I'm a guinea-pig.' 'What, what? a pig? Where's your tail?' said the little black pig. 'Please sir, no tail, I never had – no guinea-pig – no tail – no guinea-pigs have tails,' twittered Tuppenny in great alarm. 'What? what? no tails? I had an uncle with no tail, but that was accidental. Carry him to the fire, Sandy; he is cold and wet.'

Sandy lifted Tuppenny delicately by the scruff of the neck; he held his own head high and curled

Tuppenny turned and fled.

his tail over his back, to avoid treading on Tuppenny's hair. Paddy Pig scampered in front; 'What! what! we've found a new long-haired animal! Put more sticks on the fire Jenny Ferret! Set him down beside the dormouse, Sandy; let him warm his toes.'

The person addressed as Jane Ferret was an oldish person, about twelve inches high when she stood upright. She wore a cap, a brown stuff dress, and always a small crochet crossover. She filled up the tea-pot from a kettle on the fire, and gave Tuppenny a mug of hot balm tea and a baked apple. He was much comforted by the warmth of the fire, and by their kindness. In reply to questions he said his name was 'Tuppenny'; but he seemed to have forgotten where he came from. Only he remembered vaguely that his hair had been a grievance.

The circus company admired it prodigiously. 'It is truly mar-veel-ious,' said the Dormouse stretching out a small pink hand, and touching a damp draggled tress. 'Do you use hairpins?' 'I'm afraid, I'm sorry, I haven't any,' twittered Tuppenny apologetically. 'Let hairpins be provided – hair – pins,' said the Dormouse, falling fast asleep. 'I will go fetch some in the morning if you will lend me your purse,' said Iky Shepster the starling, who was pecking a hole in the turf to hide something. 'You will do nothing of the sort. Bring me my teaspoon, please,' said Jenny Ferret. The starling chittered and laughed, and flew to the top of the caravan where he roosted at night.

The sun had set. The red fire-light danced and flickered round the camp circle. The pony dozed beside the caravan, lazily whisking his long tail. Sandy was lying stretched before the fire and panting with the heat. He watched Tuppenny with bright brown eyes, through his shaggy white eyebrows. 'Tuppenny, where are you going to?' 'I have forgotten.' 'What do you intend to do with yourself?' 'I don't know.' 'Let him ride in the tilt-cart,' said Pony Billy; they were the first words that he had spoken. 'Tuppenny, will you come with us? You shall have your share of fun, and peppercorns, and sugar candy. Come with us and join the circus, Tuppenny!' cried all the little animals. 'I think I would like to, yes please, thank you,' twittered Tuppenny shyly. 'Quite right, quite right! what! what!' said the small black pig, 'Lucky you found us today; we will be over the hills and far away tomorrow.'

'Wake up, wake up! Xarifa Dormouse! get into your sleeping box. And you, Tuppenny, shall go to bed in this hamper. Good night!'

CHAPTER 3

Moving Camp

Tuppenny fell asleep at once, and slept for many hours. He awoke in the dark, and he bumped his head against the lid of the hamper. The tilt-cart was jolting and rumbling. 'Don't be frightened,' said a pleasant little voice from a neighbouring nest-box, 'we are only moving camp. Sleep again – sleep –' said the dormouse. Tuppenny stopped twittering. Presently there was a still more violent lurch; Tuppenny squeaked loudly. The cart stopped, and the black pig pushed back the canvas curtain of the hood. 'What? what? what? squeaking! twittering? at 3 o'clock in the morning? You will wake the dormouse!' 'Please – please, Mr. Paddy Pig, I dreamed I was in a ship.' 'What? what? a ship? Sea-sick, sea-sick? It's only me pulling the cart. Go to sleep again directly, little guinea-pig man!' Tuppenny obediently curled himself up in his hay bed.

When he woke again, it was broad daylight, and a bright windy morning. The caravan company was snugly encamped on a green level sward near an old stone quarry. There was a semi-circle of high gray rocks; topped with broom bushes, that swayed and bobbed in the rushing east wind. White clouds raced over-head; and Jenny Ferret's fire puffed and sputtered, in spite of comparative calm down below in the quarry. At the foot of the rocks for many years the Big Folk had been tipping rubbish; old pots and pans, fruit tins, jam pots, and broken bottles. Jenny Ferret had built a stone fireplace; she was cooking with an old frying pan, and some sardine tins; in fact, she was trying which tins would hold water with a view to carrying off a stock of cooking utensils. Paddy Pig was stirring the porridge for breakfast. Pony Billy grazed on the rough grass on the quarry bank. Sandy was nowhere to be seen.

'Wake up! wake up! Xarifa!' whistled the starling, 'wake up, new long-haired animal! My! what a mop of hair; it's full of hay seeds.' 'What, what! you meddlesome bird! His hair is beautiful! It will draw crowds when he is dressed up,' said Paddy Pig, stirring vigorously.

'If I had hair like that, I could play "Sleeping Beauty",' said the dormouse. She sat on the step

'My! what a mop of hair.'

of the caravan washing her face and hands rapidly, and cleaning her sleek chestnut coat. She had black beady eyes, very long whiskers, and a long furry tail with a white tip. Her nose and eyebrows were turning gray; she was a most sweet person, but slumberous. 'Madam, you sleep, and you are beautiful!' said Paddy Pig, turning round and bowing low, with the wooden thivel in his hand. The little fat old dormouse laughed till she shook like jelly. 'Never mind, Tuppenny; I will brush it for you. Where is Sandy?' 'Gone to buy a fiddle string, gone to buy fine clothes for Tuppenny!' whistled the starling. 'I trust he will remember hairpins. Have you a pocket-comb, Tuppenny?' 'I have no pocket, no comb, no comb, pocket-comb I forgot.' 'You appear to have forgotten most things, Tuppenny,' said Pony Billy, 'you may borrow my curry comb if it is not too large.' 'I fear it would scrape him, Pony William; but we are obliged to you. Come Tuppenny, fetch a porridge saucer and sit beside me,' said Xarifa. Tuppenny was rather silent during breakfast. He kept looking at the large print letters on the caravan. He pointed at them with his wooden spoon. 'Xarifa,' he whispered, 'is it full of polecats?' Paddy Pig rolled on the ground with laughing. 'Where is the Pigmy Elephant?' 'That's a secret,' said Jenny Ferret. 'Here, Iky Shepster, help me to tidy up. Xarifa will be busy all morning combing out those tangles.'

So then began the brushing of the hair of

Moving Camp

Tuppenny, which became a daily task. At first there were pulls and twitches and squeaks; even some hopeless tangles which had to be snipped out with Xarifa's small scissors. But after it was combed through it was easily kept in order. The brushing became a pleasure to the two little barbers. Tuppenny combed in front, and Xarifa brushed behind. Whenever the brushing stopped, Tuppenny looked over his shoulder, and discovered that Xarifa had fallen fast asleep.

She told him stories to keep herself awake; and she answered his many questions. 'Who plays the fiddle, Xarifa?' 'Paddy Pig; Sandy plays the bagpipes; and each of them does step dancing. Paddy Pig dances jigs, and Sandy dances reels; and all of us do country dances. No, no, I am not too old and fat!' said Xarifa, laughing. 'I can dance "Hunsdon House", and I can dance a minuet with Belinda Woodmouse. Perhaps we may be dancing this evening; but there is not much room in the quarry. We will soon be moving on again.' 'Do we always move in the night, Xarifa? Oh! oh! that hurts!' 'I shall have to snip it Tuppenny, give me my scissors. When we travel along the high roads we usually move in the dark; because the roads are deserted at night; very few of the Big Folk are stirring.' 'Would they chase us Xarifa?' 'No, indeed! they cannot see us, while we carry fern seed in our pockets.' 'I have not got a pocket.' 'It will be easy to plait a little packet of fern seed into your hair, like Pony Billy's. He carries one in his mane, in a plait that we call a witch's stirrup. But he once had an adventure when he lost his fern seed.' 'I did not lose it. It was stolen for mischief,' said Pony William with a snort; he was grazing near them. 'Anyway he was not invisible; he had no fern seed; so the Big Folk could see him. Now Tuppenny sit still, while I finish brushing your hair, and you shall hear the story. Only you must understand that I did not see it happen. I do not travel with the circus in winter weather. I go to live with the Oakmen.' 'Who are they, Xarifa?' 'One thing at a time. Hold your head still and listen.'

CHAPTER 4

Pony Billy in the Pound

It happened one winter there was a long spell of snow. The circus company was camping in a lonely barn. During real hard weather they usually preferred accessible places, near farms and villages; but this snowstorm had caught them unexpectedly. Indeed, the little caravan itself was fast in a snowdrift under a hedge. The tilt-cart had been dragged up to the barn, and the baggage had been carried inside. The building was dry, and fairly comfortable; but unfortunately, the great double doors could not be opened; so poor Pony Billy had to remain outside. The others, including Paddy Pig, contrived to squeeze between the upright wooden bars of an unglazed low window. There was dry bracken bedding in the barn; but no hay.

31

Pony Billy ate rough grass that grew through the snow upon the banks; he even did some digging with his forefeet, like the sheep. But when the snow continued day after day, it became necessary for him and Sandy to go foraging. They borrowed a sledge belonging to the charcoal burners, and they fetched a load of provisions; but they could only carry a very little hay as well. Pony Billy made no complaint about sleeping out. His shaggy coat was inches long; he was warm, even if he woke up half buried with snow in the morning. But he did feel as if he wanted a good feed. So one afternoon in the early darkening he announced that he intended to sup, and possibly stay a night or two, with the gypsy's donkey, Cuddy Simpson.

Sandy was not pleased. He did not mind Pony Billy going; but he – Sandy – would have liked to go, too, and spend a merry evening with Eddy Tin Cur and the gypsy lurchers.

Pony William considered the donkey a harmless, respectable animal, certainly very hardworking; but the tinker dogs were another matter. They were suspected of all manner of crimes, including sheep stealing and poaching. Therefore, he said, firmly, that it was Sandy's duty to stop with the caravan.

Iky Shepster, the starling, joined in the argument. He said people who were not sharp enough to look after their own property deserved to lose it.

32

They fetched a load of provisions.

He ran up and down on Pony Billy's back, and twitched his mane, and chittered. Pony Billy set off at dusk, walking up the lane that led to the main road. There was deep drifted snow against the walls and hedges. The lane was blocked for carts; only in the middle there was a beaten trod. The Big Folk from a farm further south had been using it; and the postman had followed it as a short cut.

Pony Billy got out onto the main road with a scramble and a jump over a frozen bank of snow, which the snow plough had cast up across the mouth of the lane. Where the plough had travelled, the road was scraped and smoother and slippery. Pony Billy walked fast without trying to trot. He picked up his neat little feet; the snow was too dry to ball in his hoofs. The night was dark, but there was a ground light from the snow. He walked forwards up the hill.

Voices came towards him on the road. Pony Billy was not concerned. The Big Folk could not see him. He had complete confidence in the fern seed which he carried. He was accustomed to walk and trot invisible. But he had not reckoned with the mischief-making of Iky Shepster. He thought that his precious packet was safely plaited into his mane; instead of which it had been stolen, and hidden by the starling in a mouse hole in the barn.

Two tall figures approached out of the darkness to meet him. Pony Billy came on, as bold as bold.

Pony Billy in the Pound

He knew that his shoes would not clink in the snow. He believed himself to be invisible; and there was plenty of room to pass. Even when he recognized that the patrollers were two very large policemen – Pony Billy still advanced.

The large policemen halted. 'What's this, Constable Crabtree?' Then at length Pony Billy stopped, too. He stood motionless; puzzled. 'It looks to me to be a large hairy black pig, Sergeant.' Pony Billy was considerably startled; but still he stood his ground. Constable Crabtree flashed a bull's-eye lantern upon him. 'It's a pony. No bigger than a big dog,' said the Sergeant. Without warning, the constable sprang at the amazed Pony William, and seized him by the forelock. Pony Billy boxed desperately; but he was overpowered by the two large policemen. And alas! the sergeant in his overcoat pocket carried a piece of strong cord, which they twisted into a rough halter.

Pony Billy threw himself down; he rolled; he kicked; he tried to bite. But all in vain! They forced him along; and the more he jibbed – the more those large policemen laughed. 'Whoa, pony! Whoa there! He is a spirited little nag! Do you recognize him, Constable Crabtree?' 'I do not, Sergeant Nutbush. There is a galloway at Hill Top Farm; but it's taller. Matter-of-fact, it's a little mare, that one; they call it Mabel.' 'Is he the pony from Swiss Cottage?' 'He is not, Sergeant. That one is a fell pony. It has nicked ears, same like a herdwick sheep; under key-bit near and cropped far.' 'Well, well, well! Put him in the Pound! Give him a bite of hay. We can advertise him in next week's Gazette.'

Pony Billy felt that things were getting extremely serious. It was so unfortunately dark; there were no other animals out upon the roads; nobody to carry news of his predicament to Sandy. It was serious.

The Pound, or Pinfold, was a round enclosure, with a high circular wall, built of cobblestones. After thoughtfully providing an armful of hay, Constable Crabtree locked up Pony Billy, and left him. The oak door was ancient, but strong. It was padlocked. The key hung upon a nail at the police station. Pony Billy had a satisfying meal at last.

Next day he tramped many, many miles, round and round inside the pinfold wall. The constable looked in, with another supply of hay, and remarked that it was funny that nobody claimed him. Pony Billy ate as much hay as he could manage to tuck in. Then he resumed his tramping round and round upon the dirty snow in the Pinfold. He neighed loudly and repeatedly. Nobody answered. The walls were very high; not the tallest Clydesdale horse could have looked over the top of those cobblestones. No living thing did he see till the second afternoon, when a small flock of starlings flew over. They wheeled round in the air, after the manner of starlings; and one bird flew

Pony Billy in the Pound

back and alighted on the wall. It was Iky Shepster. He ran along the top of the wall, and sputtered and chittered with laughter. Pony Billy ate hay and pretended not to see him. Then, just as Iky Shepster spread his wings to rejoin the flight of starlings, Pony William remarked that he wished to see Sandy on particular business. 'Is that so?' said Iky Shepster. Pony Billy was left in uncomfortable doubt whether the message would be delivered or not.

In the meantime, Sandy had no suspicion but that Pony Billy was safe with the gypsy's donkey, who spent the worst of winter eating mouldy hay and taed-pipes in an open-fronted shed on the marshes. It was a most unpleasant surprise when Iky Shepster flew in with the news that Billy was fast in the Pound. 'Whose doing is that, I wonder?' said Jenny Ferret. 'He must have lost his fern seed. I shall have to get him out somehow,' said Sandy. 'Lost, stolen, or strayed,' said Jenny Ferret. Paddy Pig suggested trying to borrow the key of the padlock from the Sergeant's black Manx cat: but it was a doubtful expedient; and it would involve calling at the police station. 'It would be simpler to pick the lock. If Mettle will only come with me we will soon have him out.'

Sandy waited till moonrise; then he scampered off to the smithy in the village. The Big Folk had all gone to bed, in the clear of the moon; but the forge was still working.

Mettle, the blacksmith's yellow terrier, was doing a job on his own; opening the links in a dog chain. Another dog was blowing the bellows. They greeted Sandy, 'Come along and warm yourself at the hearth, Sandy!' 'I'm in a hurry, I cannot wait. And you must come with me, Mettle. Poor old Billy is fast in the Pound.' 'Whew-w!' whistled Mettle. He damped down the fire, gathered up some tools, and they hurried off together.

Pony Billy was dozing in the Pinfold. He was awakened by the sound of sniffing and scratching under the door; something was being done to the padlock. Within a few minutes he was free; trotting back towards the village with the dogs racing at his heels. When the constable came next morning, the mysterious pony had vanished. The Pinfold was empty.

'So you see, Tuppenny,' said Xarifa, 'it is most important to carry fern seed when we go upon the roads, and pass near the Big Folks; and you must always take great care that it is not lost.'

CHAPTER 5

The Misses Pussycats' Shop

While the caravaners were encamped in the quarry, Sandy had gone shopping to the market town. It was an old-fashioned town with funny crooked streets and little old squares hidden away round corners; there were archways opening under houses, leading from square to square. Sandy made several small purchases at the grocer's and at the saddler's. But his most important piece of shopping was to buy something pretty to make a costume for Tuppenny, who was worthy of considerable outlay by way of dressing up. His remarkable hair, and the rarity of guinea-pigs, combined to make him an acquisition to the circus company. 'Choose something bright and fanciful; I will shape it and sew it. And pray remember hairpins!' said the

39

Dormouse Xarifa, who was clever with her needle. So Sandy in the course of his shopping paid a visit to the milliner's.

The Misses Matilda and Louisa Pussycat kept shop in a tiny steep three-storied house, with an overhanging upper floor. Each floor came forward over the story below; it made the shop rather dark for matching ribbons.

In the attic Matilda Pussycat, leaning out of the window, could talk to Tabby Whitefoot across the way, at the staircase window of the post office opposite. The street door opened down a step into the house. On the right-hand side of the passage was a tiny parlour, containing a polished mahogany table and three chairs with horse-hair seats. On a side table were the tea tray and the best tea service, and some shells and coral under a bell glass. By the fireplace were two wicker chairs with pink cushions. Some black silhouette portraits of cat ancestors hung on the wall; and on the mantelpiece stood a pot snuffbox figure, shaped like an owl. Its head took off, and the box body contained pins and buttons; not snuff. The muslin curtains were spotlessly white.

On the other side of the passage was the milliner's shop, and a dark little kitchen behind it. The Misses Pussycats lived principally in the kitchen. It was well supplied with the usual assortment of pots and pans, shelves, milk jugs, crooks for hanging things, a deal table, stools, and a corner cupboard. The only unusual feature in the kitchen was a small window under the plate rail. This window did not look out of doors like other windows; it looked into the shop. If a customer came in, Miss Louisa Pussycat applied her eye to the window, to see who it was. Once when she looked through, she saw a duck who had come into the shop without quacking.

Sandy came in from the street and lifted the latch of the shop door; it had a tinkling bell – 'Bow, wow! Shop there! Bow wow!' barked Sandy, rapping on the counter. Miss Louisa Pussycat's eye appeared at the little window. She put on a clean apron and came in behind the counter. 'Good morning, Mr. Alexander! I hope I see you well? What can I have the pleasure of showing you?' 'First rate, Miss Louisa! And how's yourself and Miss Matilda this cold weather?' 'I am very well, I thank you, Mr. Sandy; but I regret to say that my sister, Miss Matilda Pussycat, has neuralgia. A fishbone, Mr. Sandy, a fishbone embedded between her wisdom teeth; it has caused a gumboil or abscess, accompanied by swelling. She has eaten nothing but slops for a fortnight.' 'That would disagree with me,' said Sandy. 'Indeed, my poor sister Matilda is becoming as "thin as a cat's lug", as the saying is. But the spring fashions are a great divertissement and alleviation, Mr. Sandy. See here what a sweet thing in collars, Mr. Sandy; and these neckties and tabby muslins – quite the

'We can supply every requisite article of apparel.'

latest from Catchester. Is it for yourself or for a lady, Mr. Alexander?' 'Well, it's for a guinea-pig, to tell you the truth, Miss Louisa.' 'A guinea-pig! is that a species of wild boar, Mr. Sandy? Does it bite?' 'No, no! A most genteel and timid little animal, Miss Louisa. He is going to play in our circus, and we want to dress him up; something bright coloured and tasty —' 'I feel confident that we can supply every requisite article of apparel. What is his complexion? And what character will he impersonate?' inquired Miss Louisa Pussycat; she liked long words. 'He is lemon and white. We thought of calling him the Sultan of Zanzibar. How about a bandana pocket handkerchief? Can you show me any?' 'Excellent. We have a choice selection. Scarlet and gold would become him admirably. And permit me to suggest a yellow sash and a green turban; quite the height of fashion,' said Miss Louisa Pussycat, opening cardboard boxes and unwrapping packages. 'I don't think a turban would stick on, he has such a lot of hair. We were going to roll it up on the top of his head, with a hatpin stuck through it. By the bye, that reminds me, I am forgetting hairpins — hairpins with a bend in them, Miss Louisa; he has difficulty in doing up his hair.' 'Dear me, how remarkable! Cannot he have it shingled? But it would be bad for trade. You would be surprised how the sale of hairpins has diminished; we are seldom asked for them.' Miss Louisa clattered open numbers of little

43

drawers behind the counter in search of hairpins. Finally she called through the window into the kitchen – 'Sister! Sister Matilda! Where are the hairpins?' 'Miaw! miaw! oh, bother!' moaned Miss Matilda, 'I put them away in the attic; they are never wanted.' She was heard climbing the staircase.

Sandy chose a scarlet, gold and chocolate coloured pocket handkerchief, and a green sash ribbon. 'Allow me to recommend the purchase of this hatpin with a glass knob; it will shimmer in the sunshine like a diamond,' said Miss Louisa, who was greatly interested in the Sultan's costume.

Miss Matilda came downstairs with a packet of hairpins. 'Here! take them. Mi-i-a-ow! Oh, my poor mouth!' Her face was swelled like a cabbage, and she had a strip of red flannel pinned round her head. 'Let me look at it; I have had experience of bones sticking fast,' said Sandy. 'If I were sure you would not scratch me, I believe I could get it out.' 'Indeed, *I* should be thankful; she mews all night,' said Miss Louisa Pussycat. 'I'll scratch both of you if you touch me,' said Matilda. 'Matilda, this is folly. Open your mouth.' 'Louisa, I won't,' replied Matilda. 'Oh, all right; please yourself,' said Sandy. 'Will you make out my bill, Miss Louisa.' 'Let me see – half a yard of ribbon at 9 peppercorns a yard, 4½. One crystal hatpin, 7 peppercorns; one pocket handkerchief, 11 peppercorns; that makes

22½ peppercorns.' 'Miaw! You have forgotten to charge for the hairpins, Louisa.' 'Hairpins, 1½ peppercorns. That gets rid of the half. Small change is troublesome, is it not, Mr. Alexander? Twenty-four peppercorns exactly, thank you.'

'By the bye, what is the smallest size you stock in fancy slippers, Miss Louisa?' 'Kitten quarter two's, Mr. Sandy,' said Miss Louisa, reaching up towards the top shelf. 'I'm afraid that would be too large; no, don't trouble please to get them down; I know they would be too large, Miss Louisa.'

At this point Miss Matilda again mewed dismally, 'Miaw! mi-a-aw! Oh, my poor face.' 'I am out of patience with that wearisome fishbone. Sister, why will you not allow our obliging customer to examine it?' 'What do you want me to do?' asked Matilda crossly. 'Put on these wash-leather gloves so that you cannot scratch; sit back in this chair – so – now open your mouth.' Matilda opened it wide with the intention of spitting at them. Instantly Miss Louisa wedged a spoon between her jaws. 'Quick, Mr. Sandy! Get the sugar tongs off the tea tray in the parlour. That's it! Quick, before she scratches us! She is kicking her slippers off to scratch!' After a brief struggle Sandy held up the fishbone in the sugar tongs, while Matilda Pussycat made loud howls. 'Indeed, Mr. Sandy, the firm is under a great obligation to you; she had not trimmed one hat during the last fortnight; besides disturbing my rest. Pray do us the favour to accept this short length of blue ribbon, which I will enclose in your parcel as a present from us both.' 'Speak for yourself, Sister, I hate dogs!' said Matilda Pussycat, spitting and sputtering. 'Good morning, Mr. Alexander.' 'Good morning, Misses Pussycats.' And so Sandy was bowed out at the front door with his parcel. It was quite three days before the swelling disappeared; and when the Misses Pussycats had friends to tea next Saturday, the sugar tongs were discovered to be somewhat bent.

Sandy's purchases were much approved by the rest of the circus company; especially the hatpin.

CHAPTER 6

Little Mouse

Xarifa the dormouse sat upon a hazel twig that lay upon the moss; she stitched busily. She was making the gold and scarlet pocket handkerchief into a robe for Tuppenny. Tuppenny sat opposite to the dormouse, holding two sides of the handkerchief while she sewed them together. 'It is a long seam, Xarifa.' 'Shall I tell you a story to pass the time?' 'That would be lovely, Xarifa.' 'Let me see, what shall it be? I will tell you about Little Mouse.' 'Who was Little Mouse, Xarifa?' 'I don't know, Tuppenny; she was just a little mouse, and she was asked to a wedding. And she said "What shall I wear? What shall I wear? There is a hole in my old gray gown, and the shops are shut on a Wednesday." (You see, Tuppenny, it was the day

47

'There came to the door of her little house an old buff-green
striped caterpillar man.'

Little Mouse

before the wedding and the shops were not open.)
So she said – "What shall I wear? What shall I
wear?" And while Little Mouse was wondering
there came to the door of her little house an old
buff green-striped caterpillar man, with a band
across his shoulder and a pack upon his back. And
he sang, "Any tape, any buttons, any needles, any
pins? Any hooks, any eyes, any silver safety-pins?
Any ribbons, any braid, any thread of any shade,
any fine spotty muslin today, M'mm?" He turned
the band over his head and stood the pack open on
the doorstep, and showed Little Mouse his wares.
And she bought fine spotty muslin from the caterpillar man. Little Mouse spread the muslin on her
table, and she cut out a mob-cap and tippet. Then
she said "I have scissors and thimble and needles
and pins; but no thread. How shall I sew it? How
shall I sew it?"

'Then by good luck there came to the door of her
house a hairy brown spider with eight little eyes.
He, too, had a pack, a tin box on his back; and his
name was Webb Spinner. He sang "Spinneret,
spinneret! the best you can get! Reels and bobbins,
bobbins and reels! White thread and black, the
best in my pack! Come buy from Webb Spinner!"
So Little Mouse bought white thread, and she
sewed her cap and tippet. (Hold it straight please,
Tuppenny.)

'And while Little Mouse was sewing, a large
moth came to the door, selling – "Silk, spun silk!

49

Silk spun fine! Woven by the silk moth, who'll buy silk of mine?" Her silk was apple-green, shot with thread of gold and silver; and she had gold cord, and silken tassels, too. Little Mouse bought silk enough to make herself a gown, and she trimmed it with gold cord and tassels.

'And when she was dressed, attired all in her best, she said – "How can I dance? how can I dance with the Fair Maids of France, with my little bare feet?"

'Then the wind blew the grass and whispered in the leaves; and the fairies brought Little Mouse a pair of lady's slippers. And Little Mouse danced at the wedding.'

'That is lovely, Xarifa,' said Tuppenny, 'I would have liked to see the dancing. Who were the Fair Maids of France, Xarifa?' 'Little prim white flowers with white double ruffs and green stockings.' 'And the lady's slippers, were they flowers, too?' 'Yes, Tuppenny; and so are the Lambs' toes, and Lady's smocks, and Fox gloves.' 'Do foxes wear gloves, Xarifa?' 'Perhaps. But their real name is folk's gloves; fairy gloves. The good folk, the fairies, wear them.' 'Tell me about the fairies, Xarifa.' 'Another time I will, Tuppenny; my seam is finished, and Jenny Ferret is boiling the kettle for tea.'

CHAPTER 7

Springtime in Birds' Place

Spring advanced. The caravan wandered along green ways. Primroses were peeping out at the edge of the coppice; the oaks showed a tinge of gold; the wild cherry trees were snow-white with blossom. Beech trees and sycamores were bursting into leaf; only the ash trees remained bare as in midwinter. The ash is the last to don her green gown, and the first to lose her yellow leaves; a short-lived summer lady. On the topmost bare branch of an ash sat a throstle, singing loud and clear – so clear that he seemed to sing words. 'Fly here! fly here! fly here! Will-he-do-it? Will he do it?' shouted the throstle: 'Come bob-a-link, come bob-a-link! Sky high! Sky high! so – so – so.' 'Oh greenwood tree sweet pretty lea!' warbled a blackbird softly. 'Spring is here! is here!' shouted the throstle, on his tree top.

Xarifa and Tuppenny sat listening on a sunny bank below: 'Birds; sweet singers all! The coppice is full of birds. Hark to the blackbird in the hawthorn; see his yellow bill. Now he pauses, waiting for an answering blackbird, far away in the wood. It reminds me of Birds' Place in spring.' 'Where is Birds' Place, Xarifa?' 'Listen while he sings his song again.' The blackbird sang. A soft cloud dimmed the sunshine; a few large raindrops fell. The birds interrupted their singing and flew down onto the grass; all except little Dykey Sparrow, singing to his wife, while she sat on her blue speckled eggs.

'Where is Birds' Place, Xarifa?' 'Birds' Place that I remember was in Hertfordshire, long ago when I was young. Perhaps the elms and chestnuts have been felled; the passing swallows say the cedar is blown down. Birds' Place had been the garden of an old, old manor house. No brick, no stone was standing; but still the straggling damask roses bloomed, and garden flowers grew amongst the tall untidy grass. Currant and gooseberry bushes had run wild in the thicket; they bore the sweetest little berries that the blackbirds loved. No one pruned the bushes, or netted them against the birds; no one except birds gathered the strawberries that were scarcely larger than wild white strawberries of the woods. It was a paradise of birds.

Springtime in Birds' Place

'The outer side of the grove was bounded by a high close-latticed wooden fence, gray green and lichen grown; with rusty nails along the top, that kept out village boys and cats. Birds and butterflies and flowers lived undisturbed in that pleasant green wilderness that had once been a garden. And in the middle of the mossy grass plot stood the glory of the garden – the great cedar. Its head towered high above the self-sown saplings of the grove; its wide spreading lower branches lay along the mossy grass, where orange-tip butterflies flitted, and red-tailed velvety bees gathered honey from the cowslip flowers.

'Spring following spring a pair of missel thrushes built their nest upon a branch low down, and the ring doves nested and cooed higher up. Starlings and nuthatches reared their broods in holes about the trunk; the great cedar was large enough for all. The grove was carpeted with flowers, ground ivy, forget-me-nots, blue periwinkle. Amongst the bushes grew peonies and sweet-smelling day-lilies of the old garden, along with wild flowers; cow parsley, and white stitchwort that we called "milk maids", and pink ragged-robin, and cuckoo pint that is called "lords and ladies"; and everywhere primroses amongst the moss.

'There, in a nest thatched with brown chestnut leaves, I was born; I and my little dormouse sister and brother.' 'What were their names, Xarifa?' But Xarifa continued – 'Never, never anywhere have I

'In a nest thatched with brown chestnut leaves I was born.'

seen so many flowers or listened to so many birds. Even at night when it was dark, and our mother had closed up the opening of our nest with plaited leaves and grass – even in the deep black velvety darkness came the low slow note of a bird. I do not think that the nightingale's is actually sweeter than a blackbird's song; but it is weird and wonderful to hear it in the black silence of the night. There are no nightingales up here in the north, Tuppenny; but there are bonny songsters never-the-less. Father Blackbird in the hawthorn bush made me think about Birds' Place.'

'Tell me about the nest and your little dormouse brother and sister?' But Xarifa did not answer; she had fallen fast asleep, dreaming peacefully of springtime in Birds' Place.

'Tuppenny! Tuppenny!' called Jenny Ferret, 'come and help me to spread the tea things underneath the caravan; spring showers can be uncommonly wetting.' 'Tuppenny,' said Pony William, munching mouthfuls of grass between his words, 'Tuppenny do not – ask Xarifa questions about her dormouse sister and brother – she suffered from a distressing want of appetite – when she first travelled with us. It is unwise – to remind her of Adolphus.' 'I am sorry, no, yes, certainly,' twittered Tuppenny, 'I am not to, who was Adolphus, not to talk about; how many teaspoons will I fetch for you, Mrs. Jenny Ferret?' 'Only three teaspoons this time, Tuppenny; for you and me and Xarifa. Pony

Billy does not use a spoon; and Paddy Pig drinks his tea without stirring; and Iky Shepster is not here, thank goodness.' 'Where has he flown to, Jenny Ferret?' 'Up and down, and round about; scattering handbill leaves to tell the Little Folk all about our circus show tomorrow in the morning early.'

The leaves were green leaves, veined and pencilled, like as if marked by leaf-tunnelling insects; but the birds and beasts of the woods and fields know how to read them. Mice, squirrels, rabbits, and birds, as well as the larger farm animals picked up the leaves; and they knew where to look for the Circus.

CHAPTER 8

The Pigmy Elephant

Paddy Pig was an important member of the circus company. He played several parts – the Learned Pig that could read, in spectacles; the Irish Pig that could dance a jig; and the Clown in spotty calico. And he played the Pigmy Elephant. It was done in this way. He was the right elephant colour – shiny black, and he had the proper flap ears, and small eyes. Of course, his nose was not nearly long enough and he had no tusks. So tusks were shaped from white peeled sticks out of the hedge, and a black stocking was stuffed with moss for a trunk. The tusks and trunk were fastened to a bridle, which Paddy Pig wore on his head. His own nose was inside the stocking, so he could move the sham trunk a little bit. One time when there was too much moss stuffing in the stocking, Paddy Pig started sneezing, and he sneezed so violently that he sneezed the stocking off altogether. Fortunately, this happened at Fold Farm where the audience was only calves and poultry; they knew so little about elephants that they thought it was part of the performance. Paddy's thin legs were clothed with black calico trousers, long enough to hide his small feet, and he learned to walk with a slow swinging gait. His worst fault was forgetting to let his tail hang down.

Upon his back he carried a howdah made of a brightly coloured tin tea caddy. The lid was open; and inside upon a cushion sat the dormouse, as 'Princess Xarifa'. She had a doll's parasol, a blue dress and a crimson shawl; and a lace handkerchief across her nose, with her black beady eyes peeping over it (provided she was not asleep).

After Tuppenny joined Alexander and William's Circus, he rode on the elephant's neck in front of the howdah, holding on by the bridle, as Paddy Pig was slippery. Tuppenny's get-up was gorgeous as the Sultan of Zanzibar; he wore the scarlet bandana handkerchief robe, a brass curtain-ring round his neck, a green sash with a wooden sword stuck in it, and the crystal-headed pin stuck in his turban of rolled up hair; and at gala performances his whiskers were dyed pink! No one would have recognized him for the miserable, ill-used little

The Circus Show

guinea-pig who ran away from his home in the City of Marmalade.

And most audiences were completely deceived by the Pigmy Elephant. It is true there was once some dissatisfaction. It was on an occasion when other pigs were present. During the first part of the programme they behaved well. They squealed with delight when Sandy stood on his head on the back of Billy the pony; and when the pony jumped through a hoop, rolled a barrel about, and went down on one knee – the four little pigs applauded vociferously.

Pony William and Sandy went out of the ring at a canter, and disappeared under the canvas flap door of the tent. There was rather a long interval. (The fact was a brace button had come off the elephant's trousers; and Xarifa, the dormouse, who did all the mending, was sewing it on again.)

The four little pigs began to fidget and play jinks; they tickled one another and disturbed several hens and two rabbits who were sitting in the front row. Then one of them jumped up and ran to the tent, and peeped under the flap. Sandy bit his nose.

Whether because he had seen something, or because his nose smarted, it is certain the four little pigs commenced to behave badly. The entrance of the Pigmy Elephant drew exclamations of awe from the rest of the audience; but the four little pigs sniffed, and whispered together. 'I say, Mister!' said a pig to Sandy, as he stalked past, leading the elephant by a string, 'I say, Mister! What's the matter with your elephant's tail?' Sandy ignored the question; but as soon as they were out of hearing at the opposite side of the ring, he whispered to the elephant – 'Uncurl it, Paddy, you stupid! hang your tail down!' The elephant obediently allowed his tail to droop. 'I say, Mr. Elephant!' said another little pig as the procession marched round a second time – 'I say, Mr. Elephant! have a potato?' Now Paddy Pig would have liked to accept the potato which they offered to the toe of his stocking trunk, but he was quite unable to grasp it. 'There is something funny about that elephant!' exclaimed all four little pigs; and they started shouting, 'Give us back our peppercorns!' (that was their entrance money) – 'Give us back our peppercorns! We don't believe it is an elephant!' 'Do be quiet behind there!' expostulated the rabbits and poultry; 'Oh, how sweetly pretty! Look at the Princess's parasol!' The Princess Xarifa in the howdah beamed down on the admiring hens.

"That is not a proper elephant at all. Give us back our peppercorns!' shouted all four little pigs, scrambling over the turf seats into the ring, and sniffing at Paddy's calico trousers. Then Sandy lost his temper; he barked and he bit the four little pigs, and chased them out. The elephant and his riders galloped away under the tent flap in such a

60

hurry that Tuppenny and Xarifa were nearly pulled off by the canvas.

Then Jane Ferret was led round in a heavy chain and a large wire muzzle, to impersonate the 'Live Polecats and Weasels', mentioned on the posters. Jenny Ferret lived on bread and milk and she had not a tooth in her head, being, in fact, cook-housekeeper to the circus company, but the rabbits scrambled hastily into back seats. Of course that was part of the performance that they had paid for and expected; if they had not had a fright for their peppercorns, they would have been dissatisfied too. In the meantime the elephant had changed his clothes; he came back as Paddy Pig himself, and he danced a jig to perfection, while Sandy fiddled. The four little pigs, quite restored to good humour and polite behaviour, applauded loudly and threw potatoes at him; and the audience went home at 4.30 a.m. well satisfied. And two hours later the farmer, who owned the four little pigs, when he fed them, remarked – that 'For sure they were doing a deal of grunting and talking together that morning'; and there were a lot of little pig-foot-marks in the lane. But they were shut up all right in the sty when he brought them their breakfast, so he never guessed that they had been to Sandy and William's Circus to see the Pigmy Elephant.

CHAPTER 9

By Wilfin Beck

All upon a day in the month of April, the circus company crept slowly through soft green meadows. It was early morning. Long shadows from the woods lay across the grass. Birds sang to greet the rising sun. Iky Shepster, the starling, whistled and fluttered his wings on the roof of the caravan.

Pony Billy bent to the collar. The dew splashed from his shaggy fetlocks as he lifted his feet amongst the wet grass. Paddy Pig toiled between the shafts of the tilt-cart, assisted by the panting Sandy, harnessed tandem. 'We shall stick fast, Sandy! Let us go back to Pool Bridge.' 'Yap! yap! we will try the next ford higher up.' 'Get out of my way,' said Pony Billy, coming up behind them, steadily pulling the caravan.

By Wilfin Beck

They were trying to cross a stream that ran through the middle of the valley. In summer it was a little brook, but spring rains had filled it to the brim. The forget-me-nots waved to and fro, up to the waist in water; the primroses on the banks drew up their toes; the violets took a bath. Wilfin Beck was in high flood.

Paddy Pig disliked water. The ford which they should have crossed, had proved to be a swirling stream, instead of a broad rippling shallow. He wished to turn back and go round by the bridge.

The proprietors of the circus refused. 'If we cross the stream as far down as Pool Bridge, there will be two days' toilsome march through the woods. We broke a spring of the caravan last time we went by the drift road; and the wagoners have been snigging timber since then,' objected Sandy. 'Go on to the Ellers ford,' said Pony Billy. So Paddy Pig pulled, grunting, through the fast-asleep buttercups and daisies.

Xarifa and Tuppenny, in the cart, were fast asleep too. Jenny Ferret was awake inside the caravan. A pot had hit her on the head, when the wheel sank into a drain and caused the caravan to lurch.

When Tuppenny woke up and peeped out, the procession had halted, and unharnessed, beside the beck. Sandy was rolling on the grass. Paddy Pig was smoking a pipe and looking pigheaded, which means obstinate. 'You will be drowned,' said he to Pony Billy. The pony was pawing the water with his forefeet, enjoying the splashes, and wading cautiously step by step further across. 'Drowned? Poof!' yapped Sandy, taking a flying leap splash into the middle; he was carried down several yards by the current before he scrambled out on the further bank. Then he swam back. 'It's going down,' said Sandy, sniffing at a line of dead leaves and sticks which had been left stranded by the receding flood. Pony Billy nodded. 'Let us pull round under the alder bushes and wait.' 'Then you will not go back by Pool Bridge?' 'What! all across those soft meadows again? No. We will lie in the sun behind this wall, and talk to the sheep while we rest.'

So they pitched their camp by the wall, where there is a watergate across the stream, and a drinking place for cattle. Pony Billy's collar had rubbed his neck; Sandy was dog tired; Jenny Ferret was eager for firewood; everyone was content except Paddy Pig. He did his share of camp work; but he wandered away after dinner, and he was not to be found at tea time. 'Let him alone, and he'll come home,' said Sandy.

'Baa baa!' laughed some lambs, 'let us alone and we'll come home, and bring our tails behind us!' They frisked and kicked up their heels. Their mothers had come down to Wilfin Beck to drink. When their lambs went too near to Sandy, the ewes stamped their feet. They disapproved of

Eller-Tree Camp
See page 64

strange dogs – even a very tired little dog, curled up asleep in the sun.

The sheep watched Jenny Ferret curiously. She was collecting sticks and piling them in little heaps to dry; short, shiny sticks that had been left by the water.

Xarifa and Tuppenny were at their usual occupation, giving Tuppenny's hair a good hard brushing. Xarifa was finding difficulty in keeping awake. The pleasant murmur of the water, the drowsiness of the other animals, the placid company of the gentle sheep, all combined to make her sleepy. Therefore, it fell to Tuppenny to converse with the sheep. They had lain down where the wall sheltered them from the wind. They chewed their cud. 'Very fine wool,' said the eldest ewe, Tibbie Woolstockit, after contemplating the brushing silently for several minutes. 'It's coming out a little,' said Tuppenny, holding up some fluff. 'Bring it over here, bird!' said Tibbie to the starling, who was flitting from sheep to sheep, and running up and down on their backs. 'Wonderfully fine; it is finer than your Scotch wool, Maggie Dinmont,' said Tibbie Woolstockit to a black-faced ewe with curly horns, who lay beside her. 'Aye, it's varra fine. And its lang,' said Maggie Dinmont, approvingly. 'It would make lovely yarn for mittens; do you keep the combings?' asked another ewe, named Habbitrot. 'I have a little bag, there is only a little in it, yes please, I put it in a little bag,' twittered Tuppenny, much flattered by their approbation.

'Baa! baa! black sheep! Three bags full!' sang the lambs, kicking up their heels.

'Now, now! young lambs should be seen, not heard. Take care, you will fall in!' said Tibbie Woolstockit, severely. Three more ewes hurried up, and gave their lambs a good hard bat with their heads; but the lambs minded nothing.

The ewes, whose names were Ruth Twinter, Hannah Brighteyes, and Belle Lingcropper, stepped down to the water side to drink. Then they lay down by the others, and considered Tuppenny. 'His hair is as fine as rabbit wool, and longer. Rabbit wool is sadly short to spin,' said Habbitrot. 'Save all the combings in your little bag, in case you pass this way again.' 'You were not with the circus last time they camped by the Ellers?' said Tibbie Woolstockit. 'What may your name be, little guinea-pig man?' 'Tuppenny.' 'Tuppenny? a very good name,' said the sheep.

At this moment a bunch of lambs galloped across the meadow with such a rush that they nearly overran the bank into the water. Their mothers were quite angry. 'A perfect plague they are! But never-the-less we would be sad without the little dears! Now lie down and be quiet, or you will get into the same scrape as Daisy and Double!' But the lambs only raced away faster. Xarifa had been awakened by the disturbance. 'Who were Daisy

By Wilfin Beck

and Double? We love hearing stories, Tibbie Woolstockit; do tell us!'

Tibbie Woolstockit turned her mild bright eye
on the little dormouse. 'Willingly I will tell you.
There is not much to tell. Every spring for four
and twenty years we have told that story to our
lambs; but they take little heed. Daisy and Double
were the twin lambs of my great grandmother,
Dinah Woolstockit of Brackenthwaite, who grazed
in these pastures, even where we now are feeding.
The coppice has been cut thrice since then; but
still the green shoots grow again from the stools,
and the bluebells ring in the wood. And Wilfin
Beck sings over the pebbles, year in and year out,
and swirls in spring flood after the melting snow.
That April when Daisy and Double played in this
meadow, Wilfin was full to overflowing, as high as
it is now. Take care! you thoughtless lambs, take
care!

'But little heed will you take; no more than
Daisy and Double, who made of the flood a play-
mate. For it was carrying down sticks and brown
leaves and snow-broth – as the trout-fishers call
the cakes of white fairy foam that float upon the
flood water in early spring. Daisy and Double saw
the white foam; and they thought it was fun to
race with the snow-broth; they on the meadowbank
and the foam upon the water; until it rushed out
of sight behind this wall. Then back they raced
upstream till they met more snow-broth coming

down; then turned and raced back with it. But they watched the water instead of their own footsteps – splash! in tumbled Daisy. And before he could stop himself – splash! in tumbled Double; and they were whirled away in the icy cold water of Wilfin Beck. "Baa! baa!" cried Daisy and Double, bobbing along amongst the snow-broth. Very sadly they bleated for their mother; but she had not seen them fall in. She was feeding quietly, by herself. Presently she missed them; and she commenced to run up and down, bleating. They had been carried far away out of sight, beyond the wall; beyond another meadow. Then Wilfin Beck grew tired of racing; the water eddied round and round in a deep pool, and laid the lambs down gently on a shore of smooth sand. They staggered onto their feet and shook their curly coats – "I want my mammy! baa, baa!" sobbed Daisy. "I'm very cold, I want my mammy," bleated Double. But bleat as they might, their mother Dinah Woolstockit could not hear them.

'The bank above their heads was steep and crumbly. Green fronds of oak-fern were uncurling; primroses and wood anemones grew amongst the moss, and yellow catkins swung on the hazels. When the lambs tried to scramble up the bank – they rolled back, in danger of falling into the water. They bleated piteously. After a time there was a rustling amongst the nut bushes; someone was watching them. This person came walking slowly along the top of the bank. It wore a woolly shawl, pulled forward over its ears, and it leaned upon a stick. It seemed to be looking straight in front of it as it walked along; at least its nose did; but its eyes took such a sharp squint sideways as it passed above the lambs. "Burrh! burrh!" said this seeming woolly person with a deep-voiced bleat. "Baa! baa! We want our mammy!" cried Daisy and Double down below. "My little dears come up! burrh! burrh! come up to me!" "Go away!" cried Daisy, backing to the water's edge. "You are not our mammy! Go away!" cried Double. "Oh, real mammy, come to us!" Then the woolly person reached out a skinny black arm from under the shawl, and tried to claw hold of Daisy with the handle of its stick. Its eyes were sharp and yellow, and its nose was shiny black. "Baa, baa!" screamed Daisy, struggling, and rolling down the bank, away from the crook. "Burrh! burrh! bad lambs; I'll have you yet!"

'But what was that noise? A welcome whistle and shout – "Hey, Jack, good dog! go seek them out, lad!" The wily one threw off the shawl and ran, with a long bushy tail behind him; and a big strong wall-eyed collie came bounding through the coppice, on the track of the fox. When he came to the top of the bank, he stopped and looked over at Daisy and Double with friendly barks. Then John Shepherd arrived, and came slithering down the bank between the nut bushes. He lifted up Daisy

69

'The woolly person tried to claw hold of Daisy with the handle of its stick.'

and Double, and carried them to their mother. But it is in vain that we tell this tale to our lambs from generation to generation; they are thoughtless and giddy as of old. Well for us sheep that –

> 'There's sturdy Kent and Collie true,
> They will defend the tarrie woo'!'

Sing us the spinning song that the shepherd lasses sang, when they sat in the sun before the shieling, while they cleaned the tarry fleeces; carding and spinning –

'Tarrie woo', oh tarrie woo' – tarrie woo' is ill to spin,
Card it weel, oh card it weel! Card it weel ere you begin.
When it's carded, rolled, and spun, then your work is but half done,
When it's woven, dressed, and clean, it is clothing for a queen.

It's up you shepherds! dance and skip! O'er the hills and valley trip!
The king that royal sceptre sways, has no sweeter holy days.
Sing to the praise of tarrie woo'!
Sing to the sheep that bare it too!

Who'd be king? None here can tell,
When a shepherd lives so well;
Lives so well and pays his due,
With an honest heart and tarrie woo'.'

CHAPTER 10

The Sheep

The sheep lay quietly, chewing their cud. Tuppenny fidgetted, 'When will Paddy Pig come back?' '*I* don't know,' said Jenny Ferret crossly, 'I'm only an old body. I'm wanting my tea.' 'Ring the bell, Jenny Ferret,' said Sandy. She clanged a little hand-bell up and down. The lambs sprang away, startled; the sheep lay unconcerned. The sheep talked to one another. 'A bell? Sheep bells are sweeter! Ruth Twinter, do you remember the Down ram, telling us about the Cotswold flocks? How with each flock a two-three sheep go before, wearing bells? When they lift their heads from nibbling and step forward, the bells ring – ting ting ting – tong tong tong – tinkle tinkle tinkle! Why has Mistress Heelis never given us bells? She will do anything for us sheep?' 'I know not,' answered Ruth Twinter.

'I can tell you from the wisdom of age,' said the old Blue Ewe (sixteen years gone by since first she nibbled the clover); 'I can tell you. It is because we Herdwicks range singly and free upon the mountain side. We are not like the silly Southron sheep, that flock after a bell-wether. The Cotswold sheep feed on smooth sloping pastures near their shepherd.'

Said the peet ewe, Blindey, 'Our northern winds would blow away the sheep bells' feeble tinkle. From the low grounds to us comes a sound that carries further – Old John calling with a voice like a bell; calling his sheep to hay across the frozen snow in winter.'

Up spoke a dark Lonscale ewe – 'Each to their own! The green fields of the south for them; the high fell tops for us who use to wander, and find our way alone, through mist and trackless waste. We need no human guide to set us on our way.'

'No guide, nor star, nor compass, to set us a bee-line to Eskdale!' said the bright-eyed Allonby ewe (her that had knocked her teeth out when she tumbled down Scaw fell). 'Two of you Lonscales were runaways, in spite of old John's hay.' 'Who can langle the clouds or the wind? If we want to come back – we will!'

'Where was it that they drove you, Hannah Bright-eyes?' asked the little ewe, Isabel. 'Nay! I did not stay to learn its place name; I came straight back to my heaf on the fell! It was eight miles to Cockermouth market, and twelve beyond.' 'What short-wooled sheep could do that?' said Habbitrot, 'it takes strong hemp to langle us.' 'We want no bells and collars,' said Blindey, 'they would get caught on rocks and snags.' 'A sad death it must be to die fast,' said Hill Top Queenie, plaintively; 'I would not like to be fast, like poor little Hoggie in the wood. He had eaten sticks and moss as far as he could reach; but he had not sense to bite through the cruel bramble that held him, twisted round his woolly ribs.'

'Grown sheep can get crag-fast,' said Belle Lingcropper, 'I was fast in Falcon Crag. I knew each yard of slippery screes; and the chimnies, or rifts, that lead up to the high ledges. A summer drought had parched the herb; only where water oozed from the rock face, it was green. I went up and up, a hundred feet, always feeding upwards. Down below, the tree tops quivered in the heat; and a raven circled slowly. Dizziness is unknown to Herdwick sheep; I fed along a narrow ledge.

'A rock gave way beneath my feet. It clattered down into the abyss. I sprang across the gap, and went on feeding. The grass was longer; it seemed as though no sheep had bitten it. Nor had we! Our turning spot had been upon the stone that fell. I could not turn.

'I lived thirty days upon the ledge; eating the

grass to the bone; parched by the sun and wind.
Only a welcome thunder shower brought moisture
that I licked on the stones. I bleated. No one heard
me, except the raven. In the fourth week a shepherd and his dog saw me from below. He shouted;
I rose to my feet. He watched me for a time; then
he went away, and left me. Next day he came
again and shouted. I staggered along the ledge.
Again he left me; fearing that I might leap away
from him to death, if he approached too near. On
the last day, three shepherds came and watched.
I was too weak to rise; I dozed upon the ledge. They
climbed round the hillside; and they came sideways above the crag. I could hear their voices
faintly, talking overhead. One came down on a
rope; he swung inward onto the ledge, and tied
another rope to me – a woolly fleece and rattling
bones! They drew me up. Still I can feel the hot
breeze, and smell the wild sage, as they slung me
past the face of the rock. I was carried to the farm,
and given warm milk. Within a week I was well.'

'A brave shepherd, truly: one who would go
through fire and water and air to save his sheep.'

'Our shepherds face rough times,' said White
Fanny, 'dost remember hearing tell of the lad who
parted from his fellow shepherd when the early
winter sunset was going down over the snow? The
other one came home at tea time; but he did not
come. His folks turned out to seek for him; some
went along the tops; others searched below the

crags. There they saw marks of a rush; and his collie Bess watching by a snow-drift. Just in time; just and so!' 'Our men take risks with their eyes open: they know that they cannot live underneath snow like us.'

Then Ruth Twinter spoke up cleverly: 'I and three sisters were buried twenty-three days beside the Dale Head wall.' 'Nought to brag on!' said the Lonscale ewe scornfully; 'could you not feel it coming? or were the gates shut?'

'Nay, they stood open. The wind went round suddenly, after a plash of rain. A fall came out of the east. Then it turned to frost.' 'I doubt you *were* a twinter, or a two-shear at most!' said the Blue Ewe; 'the low east brings the heaviest falls.'

'Indeed, and indeed we were hurrying,' said Ruth Twinter; 'we came down the fell, strung out in single file. I mind me we met a fox at Blue Ghyll, going up. Then we met a blizzard that blew us into the wall. A blinding yellow storm of dithering powdery flakes. Belle Lingcropper's mother went over a bank into the beck; she was dashed against the stones and drowned. The rest of us cowered by the wall. We were quickly snowed over. It drifted level with the cams. We stirred ourselves under the drift, like the mowdie-warps and field voles. Our breath melted the snow somewhat; it caked over our heads, a blue green frozen vault. We ate all the bent-grass that we could reach; all the grey moss on the wall. The dogs

The Sheep

found us at last: dogs scratching, and shepherds prodding the drift with the long handles of their crooks.'

'You would feel it colder when you came out?'

'Yes,' said Ruth Twinter, 'it was warm and stuffy under the snow. Although we came out into spring sunshine, the air outside felt colder than it did inside the great white drift that lay on the grass along the Dale Head wall. We came out quite lish and cheerful. Two of us never heard the cuckoo again. Such things will happen,' said Ruth Twinter placidly, turning on her shoulder and chewing her cud. Said old Blindey, 'It is a sign of snow, when the sheep come down to the gates. Sing us the rhyme, Hannah Brighteyes:

"Oh who will come open this great heavy gate?
The hill-fox yapps loud, and the moon rises late!
There's snow on the fell, and there's hay at the farm –

Not that us elder ewes reckon much of hay; not unless we had learned to eat it while we were hoggie-lambies.'

'You had cause to be grateful to the sheepdogs, Ruth Twinter,' said Sandy. 'Yes, the dogs are our good friends. Sometimes over rough; but faithful.'

'They get crag-fast too,' said Sandy. 'They do. But they make such a fine haloobaloo! that they are more quickly found. There was one that made a bit of noise too loud. That happened in a blizzard. Poor dog, its position was so bad that it could

77

neither get down nor up; and it could not be rescued with ropes. Its master tried in vain to get it out. It cried on the shelf for several days, in sleet and biting wind; cried so pitifully that the master said he would shoot it with his own hand, before he would watch it die of cold. He went home for his gun. When he was returning with the gun – he met Collie Allen in the road!'

'All dogs are not so lucky. Our Brill's mother got cragged and killed in Langdale.' 'It is always the foremost best hound that goes over with the fox,' said Sandy; 'has Brill come back to the farm?' 'Yes,' said the sheep, 'the hunting season is over; the pack is disbanded; the hounds and terriers have gone back to the farms for the summer.' 'If all the terriers are as cross as Twig – they can stay away!' said Sandy, shaking his ears. 'Our collie Nip can tackle a fox; she has led the hounds before now, for the first short burst up the quarry pastures. She can run, can old Nip!'

'Foxes are hateful,' said Tibbie Woolstockit, stamping; 'come here, you lambs, come here! You are straying too far off.'

'Do you remember, Ruth Twinter, when you and I were feeding above Woundale; we looked over the edge into Broad How? Far down below us we could see three little fox cubs, playing in the sun. Sometimes one would grab another's tail, like a kitten; then one would sit up and scratch its ear –' ('Full of fleas,' remarked Sandy) – 'then

'The vixen was curled up asleep.'

another would roll over on its back, like a fat little puppy dog. The vixen was curled up asleep on top of a big boulder stone. Presently one of our shepherds appeared, a long way off, walking along the other side of the valley. The vixen slipped quietly off the rock; stole away over Thresthwaite Mouth into Hartsop, a mile away from the cubs. She seemed to give no sound nor signal; but the little foxes vanished into the borran.' 'Very pretty. Charming! I wonder how many lambs' tails and legs there were in the larder?' said Hannah Bright-eyes, sourly; 'they took over thirty, one spring: big lambs, too: old enough to be tailed and marked. They had skinned a lamb with Mistress Heelis' mark on its jacket. And there was part of one of Jimmy's ducks.'

'I love the high places,' said Belle Lingcropper; 'I remember, when I was a lamb, I and my brother twin were feeding on Pavey Ark with our mother. We were feeding part way up.

'Two climbing men came up, behind us and below. I do not think they knew that they were driving us before them. We climbed and climbed in the chimney that had scarcely foothold for a goat. We reached a shelf some four feet from the top. Our mother jumped out nimbly. My brother followed her with difficulty. Time and again I jumped; only to fall back upon that ledge above the precipice. Our mother bleated overhead. She moved to a spot where the wall of rock was lower.

The Sheep

I followed sideways along the ledge; looking up at her and bleating. At the third trial I jumped out. There was sweet grazing on the top.'

Cool is the air above the craggy summit. Clear is the water of the mountain keld. Green grows the grass in droughty days beneath the brackens! What though the hailstorm sweep the fell in winter – through tempest, frost, or heat – we live our patient day's allotted span.

Wild and free as when the stone-men told our puzzled early numbers; untamed as when the Norsemen named our grassings in their stride. Our little feet had ridged the slopes before the passing Romans. On through the fleeting centuries, when fresh blood came from Iceland, Spain, or Scotland – stubborn, unchanged, UNBEATEN – we have held the stony waste.

Dunmail; Faulds; Blue Joe; Wastwater Will and Thistle; Rawlins; Sworla; Wonder – old Pride of Helvellyn – pass the tough lineage forward; keep the tarrie woo' unsoftened! Hold the proud ancient heritage of our Herdwick sheep.

CHAPTER 11

Habbitrot

'Now one more tale before the sun goes down. Come Habbitrot tell us of the spinner, her that you are named after.' Habbitrot, the sheep, drew her feet beneath her comfortably, and thus commenced:

'Long, long ago, long before the acorn ripened that has grown into yonder oak – there lived a bonny lass at the farm in the dale, and a yeoman from Brigsteer came to court her.

'Her parents were willing for the match, and Bonny Annot liked the yeoman well; a brave, handsome fellow and a merry. He had sheep on the fell, kine in the byre, a horse in the stall, a dry flag-roofed house, and many a broad acre. For dower her father would give her a cow and stirk, a score of sheep, and ten silver merks.

'Her mother would give her her blessing; but not without shame and a scolding. Now this was the trouble – two elder daughters when they married had had great store of blankets and sheets. For it was a good old custom in the dale that all menseful lasses should spin flax and wool, and have the yarn woven by the webster, so that they had ready against their bridewain a big oak bedding chest well filled with linen and blankets.

'But this youngest daughter, Bonny Annot, was both the laziest and the bonniest; not one pound of wool had she carded, not one hank of tow had she spun! "Shut thee in the wool loft with thy spindle; go spin, idle Annot, go spin!"

'Bonny Annot spun from morning till noon, from noon till the shadows grew long. But it was late a-day to commence to spin. "My back is tired, my fingers are stiff, my ears they drum with the hum of the wheel. Oh well and away to Pringle Wood, to meet my love," in the gloaming. She left her wheel, she lifted the latch, she stole away while the cows were milking.

'In Pringle Wood across the beck the hazels grew as still they grow, and wind flowers and violets and primroses twinkled. Bonny Annot wandered through the wood, she knelt on the moss to gather a posey; and herself was the sweetest of flowers that grow. Blue were her eyes like the wood violet's blue, fair were her locks like the mary-bud's gold, and her red-and-white dimples like roses on snow!

She bent to the flowers and she heard a low humming. Was it horse's hoofs on the fell road from Brigsteer? Trot, trot, habbitrot, trot, trot, trot, trot, trot! She lifted her head and she listened; but no. She knelt on the moss and again she heard humming; was it bumbly bees storing their honey below? She peeped between stones and mossy hazel stumps, beneath a hollow stone, beneath a mossy stump – and there underground she saw a wee wee woman spinning – hum, hum! went her wheel; spinning, spinning, spinning.

' "Hey, Bonny Annot!" said the little gray woman, "why art thou so pale and heavy-eyed?"

' "With spinning, good woman, with spinning!"

' "Spinning is for winter nights, Bonny Annot; why spinnest thou now, in the pleasant spring?" "Because I was idle, I now must spin in haste. Alack! my sheets and blankets are to spin." She told her tale and cried.

' "Dry your eyes and listen, Bonny Annot," said the little gray woman, "eyes so blue and tender were never meant for tears. Lazy thou mayest be, but I know thee kind and true. Step up to the wool-loft in the moonlight; tie the bags of tow and wool upon the pony; bring them to old Habbitrot, and she will do thy spinning!" Even while Annot thanked her there came the clink of horseshoes along the stony road from Brigsteer; Bonny Annot forgot her troubles and sprang to meet the yeoman.

'But when he rode away next morning her

troubles recommenced – her mother, with a hazel-rod, drove her up the steps to the loft, "It wants but three weeks to thy wedding – go spin, idle daughter, go spin!" Many were the fleeces and the bags of wool and flax. So many that when she took away a load upon her pony – the wool was never missed; not although she made four journeys to and fro from Pringle Wood. "Bring more, bring more to old Habbitrot! Thou shalt have wealth of sheets and blankets!" Down below under the hollow stone there was the noise of spinning; hum, hum, trot, trot, trot! habbitrot, trot, trot!

'Little way made Bonny Annot with her own spinning in the wool-loft; yet she sang while she turned the wheel. What though the thread broke and the flax was lumpy, still she sang and laughed while she spun. In the evening she stole away once more to Pringle Wood, riding barebacked on her pony – "Lead him to the Colludie Stone! Up with the bags and bundles! Wealth for thy wedding, Bonny Annot; she that spoke kindly to old Habbitrot shall never want for blankets."

'Bonny Annot's mother expected but little in the morning. She climbed up to the wool-loft with the broomstick in her hand – "Say hast thou spun e'er a pound of wool, or a hank of tow, lazy daughter?"

'Wonders will never cease! which of her sisters had ever had such yarn for the weaver? Worsted so strong and even; or thread so fine and fair? Her fame as a spinner was spread beyond the dale; it

came to the ears of the yeoman. He, too, had great
store of white wool and flax. Said her mother, "See
what a housewife thou art marrying! Surely she
will fill thy linen-press and deck thy cupboard!"
But Bonny Annot hung her head and pouted her
lip; thought she – "He will keep me at spinning
forever."

'The wedding day came. They were a handsome
pair. The sun shone; the bells were rung; all the
folk in the dale came to the kirk to see them
married. And the wedding feast at the farm was
thronged and merry. The trenchers were piled
with meat; there were cakes and pies and pasties;
the jugs of ale went round, and Bonny Annot
kissed the cup.

'Someone knocked at the house-door. The bride
sprang to open it. At her feet upon the threshold
stood a little ugly woman, a little gray old woman,
with a kindly crooked smile.

' "Good dame, come in! Welcome to my wedding
feast!" Bonny Annot led her to the table, set chair
and footstool and cushion, filled trencher and cup.
The weddingers looked askance at the unbidden
guest; they pointed and they whispered. But still
the bonny bride served her, filling trencher and
cup. The old woman munched, and munched, and
munched. Now the bride's youngest brother was a
merry knave, "Hey, little woman!" said he, "why
hast thou such an ugly ugly mouth, wide and awry
with a long flabby lip?" "Whisht, whisht, Henry!"

said Bonny Annot, pulling him. The little woman smiled awry – "With spinning, my lad, with spinning." She wet her finger on her ugly flabby lip, and made as if she twisted thread; her thumb was broad and flat.

' "Oh ho!" said the yeoman, "is *that* what comes of spinning?" He kissed Bonny Annot's cherry lips and tapered fingers, "Oh ho! so that comes of spinning?"

'The old woman munched and munched and munched. "Hey, little woman," said Henry, "why is thy back so bent, thine eyes so bleared, and thy foot so flat?" "With spinning, my lad, with spinning!" She beat her broad foot up and down upon the flags as though she trod the treadle – trot, trot, Habbitrot, trot, trot, trot trot trot! "So ho!" said the yeoman, who was very fond of dancing, "so ho, Habbitrot! if *that* comes of spinning – my wife's foot shall never treadle. No, no, Habbitrot! When *we* have wool and flax to spin, my wife shall dance and sing. We will send for Habbitrot! Habbitrot shall do our spinning; we will send for Habbitrot." '

'That story,' said Pony Billy, 'has no moral.' 'But it is very pretty,' said Xarifa, the dormouse, suddenly wakening up.

CHAPTER 12

Across the Ford

A chill breath rose from the water. The daisies
closed their petals. 'We will say good-night,' said
the sheep, 'it is too cold for our lambs to sleep
beside the stream. Good-night, little dormouse! All
friends, good-night!' The sheep stately and peace-
ful, moved up the pasture, feeding as they went;
their lambs gambolled beside them. The last beams
of the setting sun shone again upon the flock, when
they reached the heights. Xarifa drew her fur
cloak closer. Tuppenny warmed his hands at the
fire; 'I wish Paddy Pig would come back. Do you
think he has fallen in, like the lambs?' 'Not he! he
is too much afraid of water.' Tuppenny still looked
across anxiously at the wood; 'I did think I heard
a pig squeal, while Habbitrot was telling us that

nice tale. Would anything bite him, in Pringle Wood?' Sandy sat up; 'Why did you not say so before? No, nothing would bite him.' 'I should not choose to spend a night in Pringle Wood myself,' remarked Jenny Ferret. 'Why?' inquired Tuppenny, 'why don't you like Pringle Wood? It was a kind fairy that helped Bonny Annot in the story. Does she live there yet?' 'Tuppenny,' said Pony William, 'do you not remember that I observed that the tale recounted by Habbitrot had no moral?' 'But it was very pretty,' said Xarifa, who had been to sleep again.

Supper was eaten; Tuppenny and Xarifa were put to bed; Pony Billy lay down behind the wall; Sandy went to sleep in his straw underneath the caravan – but neither at supper, at bed-time, nor at breakfast-time was there any sign of Paddy Pig.

'It is useless to wait any longer,' said Pony Billy next morning; 'the flood has gone down eight inches; we can cross the ford. If Tuppenny really heard Paddy Pig squealing in Pringle Wood, we are more likely to find him on the other side of the stream.' 'It is a mystery how he got over dry shod; and he hates getting wet,' said Jenny Ferret. 'The wood itself is a mystery,' said Pony Billy, 'we had better get through it by daylight. Xarifa, you know the reputation of Pringle Wood. Be very careful that Tuppenny does not eat anything in there.' 'Why, Xarifa?' asked Tuppenny. 'It is undesirable to taste anything that grows in the wood.' 'Is it

'I should not choose to spend a night in Pringle Wood myself.'

fairies?' 'Hush,' said Xarifa, 'we are going to cross.' 'Swim over with the rope, Sandy, and steady us.' Pony Billy took the caravan safely through the water, which was up to the axle trees. Then he unharnessed himself, and came back to fetch the tilt-cart. As there was no Paddy Pig to drag the cart, it had to be left behind for the present time, under an eller tree beside the stream on the outskirts of the wood. Tuppenny and Xarifa and the luggage were packed into the caravan to ride with Jenny Ferret.

It took them four long hours to go through Pringle Wood. Round and round and round they went, by narrow mossy tracks; always going roundabout, always pulling steadily.

And yet the wood was no great size; just a little fairy hill of oaks. The ground beneath the trees was covered with bluebells – blue as the sea – blue as a bit of sky come down. So steep downhill were the mossy banks that Sandy had to put the slipper brake under the wheel to prevent the caravan from running away on top of Pony Billy, who was nearly flung upon his nose. Then it was uphill, and Pony Billy toiled and tugged; foam flecked his bit and shoulders; his brown leather harness creaked; he was so hot with pulling that he was all in a lather. And no sooner had he gained the top of a bank than it was downhill again; just as steep, and the caravan was overrunning him, and pressing into the breeching straps.

Pony Billy snorted. His hoofs slipped on the moss; and if he left the track the bluebells were so thick that it was difficult to trample through them. They passed a bed of white anemone flowers – 'Why, surely,' said Sandy, 'we have passed this spot already, twice?'

Pony Billy snorted again, and scrambled forward. A shower of oak-apples from the trees above pelted about his ears, and rattled on the roof of the caravan. They hopped on the moss like live things; they bounced like a shower of pelting hailstones. 'Look, Xarifa! what beauties!' cried Tuppenny, trying to catch them, 'red oak-apples in April; have they been stored all winter in a wood mousey's cupboard?' 'Throw them away, Tuppenny!' exclaimed Xarifa and Jenny Ferret, 'throw them away over your left shoulder!' More and more oak-apples came pattering and pelting; Tuppenny played ball with them, catching them and tossing them back. 'This one has been bitten, Xarifa; are they good to eat?' 'What is that I hear?' said Pony Billy, laying his ears back, 'none of you on any account may eat anything that grows in Pringle Wood.' Instantly another pelting shower of oak-apples came rattling like a hailstorm about Pony Bill's mane and back. He broke into a gallop, trampling through the bluebells; and this time he succeeded in dragging the caravan clear away out of Pringle Wood.

The sunshiny open meadow was refreshing after

the sombre shade of the trees. Cattle and sheep were feeding peacefully; lambs frisked; swallows skimmed low over the buttercups that powdered Pony Billy's hoofs with dusty gold. He drew the caravan across the cheerful green grass – he took it through a white gate into a lane, which they followed down to Codlin Croft Farm.

It was a pleasant sunny spot, where the circus had camped before. 'Only it is rather too near the world of the Big Folk, and their cats and dogs and hens and cocks – especially cocks,' said Sandy, stiffening his tail.

'There is no help for it,' said Pony Billy, 'we cannot proceed further, and leave Paddy Pig behind us, lost. Besides I must go back for the tilt-cart.' Tuppenny twittered dolefully, 'You will be lost, too, Mr. Pony William!' 'I shall not,' said Pony Billy, 'I am not a pig-headed fool of a pig!' 'Now Xarifa and Tuppenny,' said Sandy, 'come along! I am sorry to say you will have to be shut up all the time while we stop at Codlin Croft. It will not be safe to let you out, with all these strange dogs and cats – here they come! Cows, calves, dogs, cats, poultry – all the farm animals!'

CHAPTER 13

Codlin Croft Orchard

The homestead of Codlin Croft was dominated by Charles, our cock, a silver campine with handsome white neck hackles, finely barred and spotted breast, and a magnificent tail. He also had a big red comb; and spurs. Besides Charles there was a turkey cock of large size; and a sow still larger; and a cat and three farm dogs. Charles treated them all alike with contempt. When the caravan arrived in the lane, Charles and the turkey were having one of their usual combats. Charles was dancing round and churtling – cluck cur-cuck-cuck-cuck! jumping and spurring at Bubbly-jock's painfully red wattles and tassels. The turkey was bursting with rage; he scrunched the tips of his wings along the gravel (which spoilt nothing but his own feathers). Whenever he got a chance he trod heavily upon the spot where Charles had recently stood. Charles, in the meantime, had darted between the turkey's legs. When Charles became short of breath, he slipped nimbly through the narrow bars of an iron gate, and pretended to be picking up titbits, in full view of the maddened turkey cock, who was unable to follow him. Then he scratched up dirt, and crowed. Charles and Sandy never hit it off very well; they both had a habit of scratching up the earth, and they mutually irritated one another. But all the same, Charles graciously did the honours of Codlin Croft, and invited the company into the orchard through a broken gate.

The orchard which gives Codlin Croft Farm its name is a long rambling strip of ground, with old bent pear trees and apple trees that bear ripe little summer pears in August and sweet codlin apples in September. At the end nearest to the buildings there are clothes-props, hen-coops, tubs, troughs, old oddments; and pigsties that adjoin the calf hulls and cow byres. The back windows of the farmhouse look out nearly level with the orchard grass; little back windows of diamond panes not made to open. The far end of the orchard is a neglected pretty wilderness, with mossy old trees, elder bushes, and long grass; handy for a pet lamb or two in spring, and for the calves in summer.

At this time of year, a north country April, the

pear blossom was out and the early apple blossom was budding. The snowdrops that had been a sheet of white – white as the linen sheets bleaching on the drying green – had passed; and now there were daffodils in hundreds. Not the big bunchy tame ones that we call 'Butter-and-eggs,' but the little wild daffodillies that dance in the wind. Through the broken gate at top of Codlin Croft orchard came Pony Billy with the caravan. He drew it up comfortably in shelter of Farmer Hodgson's hay-stack, which stood, four-square and prosperous, half in the orchard and half in the field. 'Only, Jenny Ferret, if I put the caravan here you must promise not to light a fire. We must not burn Farmer Hodgson's hay for him.' 'And how will I boil the kettle without a fire? Take us further down the orchard near the well, behind the bour-tree bushes.' 'All right,' agreed Pony Billy, pulling into the collar again; 'perhaps it would be safer. I can come up to the stack by myself for a bite.'

'Cluck-cur-cuck-cuck!' said Charles, 'I recommend that flat place between the pig-sty and the middenstead.' 'Yes, indeed, cluck, cluck! there are lots of worms if you scratch up the manure,' clucked Selina Pickacorn. 'Are they going to put up a tent?' asked the calves. 'Oh, yes, lots of nice red worms,' clucked Tappie-tourie and Chucky-partlet. 'What's that funny old woman they call Jenny Ferret? she has got whiskers?' asked an inquisitive cat, sitting on the roof of the pig-sty.

The Fairy Hill of Oaks
See page 118

Codlin Croft Orchard

'Quack, quack! stretch your long neck and peep in at the window, Dilly Duckling.' 'I cannot see; quack quack; I cannot see anything through the curtains.' 'Gobble-gobble-gobble!' shouted the turkey cock, strutting after Charles. Sandy curled his tail tightly; 'Go further down beyond the bour-tree bushes, Pony William, further away from the farmyard.' When the caravan had been drawn into position, it became necessary for Sandy to do a large loud determined barking all round, in order to disperse the poultry.

After pitching camp in the orchard Pony Billy and Sandy held an anxious consultation, 'Did you notice anything while we were coming through the wood?' 'Yes. Pig's trotter marks.' 'How many times did we go round and round that hill, Pony William?' 'We would be going round it yet, if I had not gone widdershins.' 'What shall we do about Paddy Pig?' 'I am going back to fetch him.' 'What! into Pringle Wood?' 'Yes,' said Pony Billy; 'but first I want a saddle and bridle. And look whether my packet of fern seed is safe; for I shall have to go amongst the Big Folk in broad daylight.'

Pony Billy borrowed several things, by permission of the farm dogs, Roy, Bobs, and Matt, who were lying lazily in the sun before the stable door. He asked for the loan of a nosebag containing chopped hay, and straw, and uveco; also for two pounds of potatoes; and a saddle and bridle, and for the chest-strap with brass ornaments belonging to the cart

Roy, Bobs, and Matt were lying lazily in the sun.

harness. There were four brass lockets on the strap; a swan, a galloping horse, a catherine wheel, and a crescent. The last named is a charm that has been worn by English horses since the days of the crusaders. The strap was too long; it swung between his knees; but Pony Billy felt fortified and valiant. 'Do you think you will be chased?' asked the dogs. 'I shall not. I am going to smithy to have my shoes turned back to front.' 'Our mare Maggret is at the smithy,' said Bobs. 'You will have to go past the back door and the wash-house if you want potatoes,' said Matt. 'Nobody can see me,' said Pony Billy. He clattered across the flags, bold in possession of fern seed and invisibility. Mrs Hodgson, inside the house, called to her maid-servant, 'Look out at the door, Grace; is that the master I hear coming home with the mare?' 'I hear summat, but I see nought,' answered Grace, perplexed.

Pony Billy started on his quest. The farm dogs went to sleep again in the sun.

Sandy with his tail uncurled trailed back disconsolately to the orchard camp. The ducks and calves had wandered away; but Charles and his inquisitive hens were still in close attendance, and conversing endlessly.

The conversation was about losing things. Xarifa's scissors were missing. Jenny Ferret as usual suspected Ikey Shepster, the starling. He was not present to deny the charge; he had flown off foraging with the sparrows.

'I am going to the smithy to have my shoes turned back to front.'

Codlin Croft Orchard

'Losses,' said Charles, sententiously, 'losses occur in the best regulated establishments. Likewise finds; but finds are less frequent; and, therefore, more noteworthy. One afternoon I and my hens were promenading in the meadow. I heard Tappie-tourie – that bird with the rose comb – clucking loudly in the ashpit. I inquired of Selina Pickacorn whether Tappie-tourie had laid an egg? Selina replied that it seemed improbable, as Tappie-tourie had already laid one that morning in the henhouse. But hens are fools enough to do anything; I ordered Selina to proceed to the ashpit, to ask Tappie-tourie whether she had laid a second egg or not. When one hen runs – all the other hens run too; being idiots; cluck-cur-cuck cuck cuck!' 'Oh, Charles! Charles!' remonstrated Selina and Chucky-partlet coyly. 'Aggravating idiots,' repeated Charles, who did not believe in encouraging pride amongst female poultry. 'As the whole of my hens continued to cluck in the ashpit in total disregard of my commands to come out – I stalked across the field, and I looked in. I said, "What are you doing, Tappie-tourie? you are a perfect sweep. Selina Pickacorn, you are equally dirty. Chucky-doddie, you are even worse. Come out of the ashpit." They replied, all clucking together – "Oh, Charles! do look what a treasure we have found! But none of us know how to stick it on, because it has no safety-pin." They showed me Mrs Hodgson's big cairngorm broach that had been missing for a fortnight. They asked me if it was worth a hundred pounds. Cock-a-doodle-doo! A hundred pounds, indeed!' said Charles, swelling with scorn. 'I told them it was absolutely worthless to us who wear no collars; not worth so much as one grain of wheat; cluck-cur-cuck cuck cuck! Hens always were noodles, and always will be. Ask them to tell you the tale of the demerara sugar.'

'That?' said Selina Pickacorn, quite unabashed, 'oh, that happened long ago when we were inexperienced young pullets. Besides, it was all along of the parrot.' 'Pray explain to us the responsibility of the parrot?' said Sandy. Five or six hens all commenced to cluck at once. Charles interjected cock-a-doodles. Consequently their explanation became somewhat mixed. Therefore it must be understood that this story – like the corn in their crops – is a digest.

CHAPTER 14

Demerara Sugar

Upon fine days in spring the parrot's cage was set out of doors upon top of the garden wall, opposite the farmhouse windows. In the intervals of biting its perch and swinging wrong-side up, the parrot addressed remarks to the poultry in the yard below. The words which it uttered most frequently in the hearing of those innocent birds were, 'Demerara sugar! demerara sug! dem, dem, dem, Pretty Polly!' The chickens listened attentively.

When the chickens were feathered, they were taken to live in a wooden hut on wheels in the stubble field. They picked up the scattered grain; and grew into fine fat pullets. In autumn the farmer talked of taking the hen-hut home. But he was busy with other work; he delayed till winter.

In the night before Christmas Eve there came a fall of snow. When Tappie-tourie looked out next morning the ground was white. She drew back into the hut in consternation. Then Selina Pickacorn and Chucky-doddie looked out. None of them had ever seen snow before; they were April hatched pullets without a single experienced old hen to advise them.

'Is it a tablecloth?' asked Chucky-doddie. They knew all about tablecloths because they had been reared under a hen-coop on the drying green. They had been scolded for leaving dirty foot-marks on a clean tablecloth which was bleaching upon the grass.

The hens slid nervously down the hen ladder on to the snow. No; it was not a tablecloth. Said Tappie-tourie, 'I'll tell you what! I do believe it is the parrot's demerara sugar!' (Now the parrot ought to have told them that demerara sugar is *not* white.) Selina Pickacorn tasted a beakful. 'It is nothing extra special nice; he need not have talked so much about it.' 'How horribly cold and wet it feels.' Just then the farmer came into the field with a horse and cart. He drove the hens back into the hut, fastened the door with a peg, and tied the hut behind his cart with a rope in order to drag it homewards through the snow.

The hen-hut did not run smoothly; it had a

tiresome little waggling wheel at one end, that caught in ruts. It bumped along; and the pullets inside it cackled and fluttered. Before the procession had got clear of the field – the hut door flew open. Out bounced Tappie-tourie, Chucky-doddie, Selina Pickacorn, and five other hens. The farmer and his dog caught five of them, none too gently. But the three first-named birds flew back screaming to the spot where the hen-hut had stood originally, before it had been removed.

The farmer was obliged to leave them for the present.

Tappie-tourie, Chucky-doddie, and Selina wandered around in the snow; the field seemed very large and lost under its wide white covering. 'The hut is gone,' said Tappie-tourie, with a brain wave. 'That is so,' agreed Selina Pickacorn, 'we fell out of the hut.' 'What shall we do?' asked Chucky-doddie. 'I see nothing for it but a Christmas picnic,' said Tappie-tourie; 'here is sugar in plenty, but where is the tea and bread and butter?'

Large flakes of snow commenced to fall. 'Perhaps this is the bread and butter coming,' said Tappie-tourie, looking up hopefully at the darkening sky. 'My feather petticoat is getting so wet,' grumbled Chucky-doddie; 'let us try to walk along the top of that wall, towards the wood.' The wall had a thick white topping of snow; it proved to be a most uncomfortable walk, with frequent tumblings off. They crossed Wilfin Beck on a wooden

105

rail. The water below ran dark and sullen between the white banks. By the time they had reached the wood it was dusk; for the last hundred yards the hens had been floundering through snow-drifts. 'If this is a Christmas picnic – it is horrid! Let us get up into that spruce tree, and roost there till morning.' They managed to fly up. They perched in a row on a branch, fluffing out their feathers to warm their cold wet feet. They were one speckled hen and two white hens; only the white hens looked quite yellow against the whiter snow. 'The picnic is a long time commencing,' said the speckled hen, Tappie-tourie. It was soon black as pitch amongst the spreading branches of the spruce.

Down below in the glen the waters of the stream tinkled through the ground ice. Now and then there was a soft rushing sound, as the wet snow slipped off the sapling trees that bent beneath its weight, and sprang upwards again, released. Far off in the woods, a branch snapped under its load, like the sound of a gun at night. The stream murmured, flowing darkly. Dead keshes, withered grass, and canes stood up through the snow on its banks, under a fringe of hazel bushes.

Between the stream and the tree where the hens were roosting, there was a white untrodden slope. Only one tree grew there, a very small spruce, a little Christmas tree some four foot high. As the night grew darker – the branches of this little tree became all tipped with light, and wreathed with icicles and chains of frost. Brighter and brighter it shone, until it seemed to bear a hundred fairy lights; not like the yellow gleam of candles, but a clear white incandescent light.

Small voices and music began to mingle with the sound of the water. Up by the snowy banks, from the wood and from the meadow beyond, tripped scores of little shadowy creatures, advancing from the darkness into the light. They trod a circle on the snow around the Christmas tree, dancing gaily hand-in-hand. Rabbits, moles, squirrels, and wood-mice – even the half blind mole, old Samson Velvet, danced hand-in-paw with a wood-mouse and a shrew – whilst a hedgehog played the bag-pipes beneath the fairy spruce.

Tappie-tourie and her sisters craned forward on their branch. 'Is the Christmas picnic commencing? May we fly down and share it? Shall we, too, join the dance?' They slid and sidled forward, shaking down a shower of melting snow and ice. 'Cluck, cluck!' cackled the hens, as they clutched and fluttered amongst slippery boughs.

The lights on the Christmas tree quivered, and went out. All was darkness and silence. 'I'm afraid the Christmas picnic was only a dream; we shall have to roost here till morning.' 'Hush! sit still,' said Tappie-tourie, 'it was not us that frightened them away. Something is stirring near the stream! What is it?' The moon shone out between the clouds, throwing long shadows on the snow; shadows of the hazels and tall keshes. A little figure, questing and snuffling, came out into the moonlight: a small brown figure in a buttoned-up long coat. He examined the footsteps on the snow round the Christmas tree. Then, horrible to relate! he came straight up the snowy slope and stood under the spruce; looking up at the hens. He was a disagreeable fusky musky person, called John Stoat Ferret. (At this point Charles thought it necessary to apologize to Jenny Ferret who was knitting on the caravan steps. She accepted the apology in good part, and said of course she was not answerable for disagreeable relations – a horrid fusky musky smelly relation, with short legs, and rather a bushy tail.) First he tried to climb the tree, but he could not do so. Then he cried, 'Shoo! shoo!' and threw sticks at the hens. And then he butted against the tree, and tried to shake them down. They clung, cackling and terrified, in the boughs high over head.

Then John Stoat Ferret thought of another plan; he determined to make them dizzy. He set to work. He danced. It was not at all nice dancing. At first he circled slowly; very, very slowly; then gradually faster, faster, faster, until he was spinning like a top. And always a nasty fusky musky smell steamed upwards into the tree. Tappie-tourie, Chucky-doddie, and Selina Pickacorn, overhead, watched him. They had left off clucking; they watched him in fascinated terrified silence, craning over their branch. And still he spun round and round and round, and the fusky smell rose up into the spruce. Tappie-tourie twisted her head round, following his movements as he danced. And Chucky-doddie twisted her neck round. And Selina Pickacorn not only twisted her head, she began to turn round herself upon the branch. All the hens were growing giddy.

John Stoat Ferret danced and spun more furiously, the fusky musky smell rose higher. All three hens commenced to turn round dizzily. In another minute they would fall off. John Stoat Ferret capered and twirled. But all of a sudden he stopped. He sat up, motionless, listening. Voices were approaching up the cart road that skirts the wood.

Upon Christmas Eve it is a pleasant custom amongst the Big Folk for carol singers to go singing from farm to farm; even to the lonely cottages on the outskirts of the great woods.

Two small boys, who had been out with the carollers, were going home to supper. Their Christmas picnic had been more prosperous than poor Tappie-tourie's. Their pockets were full of apples and toffy and pennies.

'George,' said Jimmy, 'give us a ginger snap.'

'Na-a!' said George, 'it will gummy your teeth tegidder, that you cannot sing. Whooop!' shouted George, jumping into a snowdrift, 'sing another –

"Wassail, wassail! to our town!
  The bowl is white, and the ale is brown;
  The bowl is made of the rosemary tree, and so is the ale,
    of the good barlee.
  Little maid, little maid, tirl the pin!
  Open the door, and let us come in!"

John Stoat Ferret listened intently. 'Whooop!' shouted Jimmy, kicking the snow about, and swinging his candle lantern; 'sing another one –

"Here us comes a wassailing, under the holly green,
  Here us comes a wandering, so merry to be seen.
  Good luck good Master Hodgin, and kind Mistress also,
  And all the little childer that round the table go!
  Your pockets full of money, your cupboards of good
    cheer,
  A merry Christmas, Guizzards, and a Happy New
    Year!"

'Jimmy!' exclaimed George suddenly, 'I smell stoat. Look over the wall with the lantern.' John Stoat Ferret departed hurriedly. And as if a spell were broken, Chucky-doddie, Tappie-tourie, and Selina found their voices. They cackled loudly, up in the tree. 'Eh, sithee!' said George, 'them's our three hens that father lost out of t' hen-hut. Fetch 'em down: I'se haud lantern.' 'This wall's gaily slape!' giggled Jimmy, balancing himself on the slippery top stones. He reached up into the tree, and got hold of Tappie-tourie first, by the legs. 'Ketch!' said he, and flung her out into the snow-drift in the lane. 'Here's another fat 'un!' He threw

110

Chucky-doddie across. Selina flew after them of her own accord. The boys picked the hens out of the snow, and trudged homewards; George, with a hen tucked under each arm; and Jimmy, with one hen and the candle lantern. It was an inglorious ending to Tappie-tourie's Christmas picnic; but at one time it looked like ending much worse – 'very much worse, Cluck-cur-cuck-cuck-cluck!' said Charles the cock.

Sandy looked thoughtful. 'Was the parrot an elderly bird?' 'Very aged by his own account, if truthful,' replied Charles.

'I wonder whether he was the same parrot who had an adventure with a hawk, long ago. The parrot, which I am referring to, belonged to Squire Browne of Cumberland. The Squire also had a chestnut cob on which he went out riding; and he employed an old groom-gardener, named John Geddes. When Squire Browne came downstairs on fine mornings, he called through the open staircase window to John Geddes in the stable-yard. He said, "I'm riding today, John Geddes!" Then he scratched the parrot's head, and read the news-paper, and had breakfast.

'Now the parrot was so tame that he was allowed to come out of his cage; and one day he was waddling about on the lawn, when – shocking to say – a large hawk swooped down from the sky, and seized poor Polly in its claws. The hawk rose into the air, over the house and stableyard; and

The boys picked the hens out of the snow, and trudged homewards.

the parrot, looking down for the last time at its home, saw the old groom-gardener sweeping with the yard broom. "I'm riding today, John Geddes!" shouted Polly. Whereupon the hawk was so startled that it let go the parrot, who skimmed downwards from the clouds to safety.'

'Cuck, cuck, cluck! I think I have heard that anecdote before,' said Charles. 'Possibly,' replied Sandy, bristling up his moustache, 'possibly. But Squire Browne's parrot was the first one it happened to.' Xarifa intervened hastily, in the cause of peace, 'Was it not Miss Browne, a very, very old lady, who told us the story?' 'It was,' said Sandy, eyeing Charles, the cock. 'And did she not tell us other pretty stories?' continued Xarifa, 'the story of the fairy clogs; and that pretty tale about the water-lilies? How they went adrift and sailed away, along the lake and down the river? In each water-lily flower was a fairy sitting, with golden curls, in the white lily flowers; and a fairy in green, on each broad round leaf, rowing with oars made of rushes?' 'What was the end of that story, Xarifa?' asked Tuppenny. 'Unfortunately, I do not remember. I don't think it had any end; or else I fell asleep.'

CHAPTER 15

Pony Billy's Search

Whilst Sandy and the poultry were entertaining each other in the orchard, Pony Billy, saddled and bridled, trotted away in search of the truant Paddy Pig. He passed in front of the farmhouse windows, clink! clink! went his shoes on the cobblestones in the yard. Mrs. Hodgson darning stockings in the sunny window-seat looked up and listened. Nothing could she see; she threaded her needle in and out, out and in, through the stocking foot. Pony Billy passed by the sweet-smelling wallflowers in the old-fashioned garden, where beehives, all a-row, stood on a deep stone shelf of the wall that faced the sun. The bees were stirring busily after their drowsy winter's sleep. He came along a cart-track, and through a gate, on to the public road.

Pony Billy's Search

Little sunshiny whirly winds had powdered white dust upon the king cups under the hedge; belated March dust in April. The cows looked over the hedge at Pony Billy. Said White-stockings to Fancy, 'There goes a brave little saddle pony! Look how proudly he arches his neck, and tosses his cunning head! See the brass lockets glittering in the sun, and the stirrup irons, and the saddle leather. Look at his long flowing tail; and how gaily he picks his steps! He lifts his feet as prettily as Merry-legs or Cricket, who won the prize at Helsington.' 'Where is he trotting to, think you?' said Buttercup Cow to Nancy. Pony Billy trotted along. It was dinner time with the Big Folk. He met nobody except old Quaker Goodman, jogging leisurely homeward in a low two-wheeled tub. The fat Quaker pony could see Pony Billy in spite of fern seed; it swerved across the road to leave him room to pass. Old Mr. Goodman laid his whip very gently along the ribs of the fat pony, as it were patting her with the handle of the whip, 'What Daisey! Why, Daisey? What is thee shying at, Daisey? Tch-tckk-tckk!' Staid iron-gray Daisey plodded steadily on; her thick bob-tail swung from side to side.

Horses can see things where the Big Folk can see nothing – nothing but a silly white stone, or a stump on the roadside bank. But horses can see. So likewise can little young children. Two toddling youngsters at play in the dust caught a fleeting glimpse of the fairy pony; they prattled baby talk, and clapped their dirty chubby hands. Pony Billy breasted the hill at a canter; he slackened his pace to a walk as he came along over the croft. He pricked his ears and looked down at the village. The Big Folk were all indoors at dinner. Maggret, the Codlin Croft mare, dozed under the pent-house at the smithy. Farmer Hodgson was gossiping at the inn, whilst he waited for the blacksmith.

Pony Billy came down the croft at a quick, high-stepping trot; his brass lockets shone in the sun; his bright eyes sparkled. He hailed the smithy with eager neighings, 'Hinny ho! Mettle! Bellows and shoes, Mettle! Hinny ho!'

Out came Mettle, barking; a hard-haired yellow terrier, wearing a little leather apron, 'Good-day to you, Pony Billy! So the caravan is round again? What can I do for you this time? Another hoop? Another new circus trick?' 'I wish to have my shoes removed and put on backwards.' 'Certainly; four removes; we will soon have them off,' said Mettle, 'it does not sound very comfortable; but just as you please. I will blow up the fire (c-r-e-a-k, puff; Mettle leaned upon the handle of the bellows, c-r-e-a-k, puff, puff), they will require a little fitting. (Mettle turned the shoe upon the hearth amongst the small hot coal, puff, puff.) I will take it out in tickets; and treat our smithy cat to an outing (puff, puff!). I owe her one. I pulled her tail. She did scratch me (puff, puff)! Why did I do it? (C-r-e-a-k, puff, puff!) I did it because she was black. I thought she was a stray black cat! She went up the chimney tortoise-shell and white, and she came down black! Cheesebox, our smithy cat.'

Farmer Hodgson's mare yawned dismally. 'I am sorry, Maggret, I cannot offer to fit your shoes; your feet are so large I could not lift them.' (The mare laid her ears back.) 'No offence to a lady! My master says he likes a horse with a big open foot.'

Mettle took the white-hot horseshoe from the hearth with a little pair of tongs and hammered it daintily on the anvil; 'Now your shoes are little fairy shoes, Pony Billy'; tick, tock, tap, tock! hammered Mettle merrily and sang, 'Shoe the horse and shoe the mare, but let the little colt go bare! Now lift up your foot till I fit it. Have you ever gone short of fern seed since that night in the snow, Pony Billy?' 'Never,' said Pony Billy, shaking his mane to feel the precious packet nestling against his neck. Tap, tap, tap! hammered Mettle, 'Here a nail and there a trod; now the horse is well shod! Yes, Cheesebox and I will be coming to the circus this evening.'

Then Maggret pricked her ears and whinnied at sound of hob-nailed boots; her master and the blacksmith came into the pent-house together. Just then Pony Billy came out. Farmer Hodgson did feel as though he had bumped against something soft; but there was nothing to be seen. It might have been the door-post.

Pony Billy walked up a stony lane picking his footsteps carefully. It is not agreeable to trot amongst stones with four newly-shod back-to-front shoes. He stepped in the softest places. By banks and hollows and turnings, by muddy places and dry, always leaving back-to-front horseshoe marks behind him, as though he had come down the lane, instead of having gone up. He turned into another lane, crossed a shallow ford; came roundabout behind the wood, and looked over a tumble-down wall.

Pringle Wood lay before him, silent, still; crowned with golden green in a pale spring afternoon. Almost silent, almost still; save for a whispering breath amongst the golden green leaves, and a faint tingle ringle from the bluebells on the fairy hill of oaks. How blue the bluebells were! a sea of soft pale blue; tree behind tree; and beneath the trees, wave upon wave, a blue sea of bluebells. Below the low stone wall, between it and the wooded hill, was a tangly boggy dell, matted with brambles and wild raspberry canes, and last year's withered meadow-sweet and keshes. Young larch trees and spruces struggled through the briars; a little stream slid gently round the hill, beneath ellers and hazel bushes.

Pony Billy came over a gap in the wall, and pushed his way through the tangle, leaving back-to-front footsteps as he squelched through the black earth and moss. Briars tugged his mane; raspberry canes pulled his tail as though they were fingers; he left tufts of his shaggy coat upon the brambles. He whinnied, 'Hinny ho! where are you hiding, Paddy Pig?' No one answered. Only there seemed to be a faint tingle ringle of laughing from the thousands of bluebells in the wood.

Pony Billy got out of the bog with a jump and a scramble up the steep grassy slope of the hill. Round and round and round he went underneath the oaks; always going widdershins, contrary to the sun; always leaving back-to-front misleading marks behind him. Six times round he went; and he saw nothing but the bluebells and the oaks. But the seventh time round he saw a little Jenny Wren, chittering and fussing round an old hollow tree. 'What are you scolding, you little Jenny Wren?' She did not stay to answer; she darted through the wood twittering gaily. 'I had better go and look inside that hollow tree myself,' thought Pony Billy. He walked up to it, and looked in. 'Ho, ho! what are you doing in there, Paddy Pig? Come out!' 'Never no more,' replied Paddy Pig. He was sitting huddled up inside the tree, with his fore-trotters pressed against his tummy; 'never again. I cannot break through the ropes.' 'Ropes? don't be silly! there is nothing but cobwebs.' 'What, what? no ropes?' 'Come out at once,' said Pony William, stamping. 'I am ill,' replied Paddy Pig; he pressed his trotters on his waistcoat. 'What have you been eating?' 'Tartlets.' 'Tartlets in Pringle Wood! more likely to be toadstools. Come out, you pig; you are keeping the circus waiting.' 'Never no more shall I return to the go-cart and the caravan.' Pony Billy thrust his head through the spider webs in the opening, seized Paddy Pig's coat-collar with his teeth, and jerked him out of the tree. 'What, what? no ropes? but it is all in vain.' He sat upon the grass and wept. 'Try a potato? I brought you some on purpose.' 'What, what? potatoes! but is it safe to eat them?' 'Certainly it is,' said Pony Billy, 'they did not grow in Pringle Wood. Eat them while I have my nosebag. Then I will carry you home again pig-a-back.' 'We will be chased. And I will fall off.' He ate all the potatoes; 'I feel a little better; but I know I will fall off. Oh, oh, oh! Something is pinching my ears!'

Whatever might be the matter, Paddy Pig's behaviour was odd. He got up on a tree-stump, and he tried to climb into the saddle. First he climbed too far and tumbled over the other side; then he climbed too short and tumbled; then he fell over the pony's head; then he slipped backwards over the crupper, just as though someone were pulling him. He sat upon the ground and sobbed, 'Leave me to my fate. Go away and tell my friends that I am a prisoner for life in Pringle Wood.' 'Try once more. Sit straight, and hold on to the strap of lockets,' said Pony Billy, trampling through the bluebells.

He came out from under the trees into the sunshine. He trotted across the green grass of the open meadow, and carried Paddy Pig safely back to camp.

CHAPTER 16

The Effect of Toadstool Tartlets

It was four o'clock of the afternoon when Pony
Billy trotted into Codlin Croft orchard with Paddy
Pig. Sandy and the farm dogs barked joyfully; the
turkey cock gobbled; Charles crowed; and Jenny
Ferret waved a dishcloth on the caravan steps.
Even Tuppenny and Xarifa – dolefully confined in
hampers – clapped their little paws in welcome.
Paddy Pig took no notice of these greetings. He
slid from the saddle, and sat by the camp fire in a
heap.

'He looks poorly,' said Sandy, anxiously, 'fetch a
shawl, Jenny Ferret.' 'Ill; very ill,' said Paddy Pig.
They wrapped him in the shawl and gave him tea;
he was thirsty, but he had no appetite. The raw
potatoes appeared to have disagreed, on top of the

tartlets. As evening closed in, he shivered more and more. The company plied him with questions – how did he get across the water into Pringle Wood? 'Over a plank.' 'I don't remember any plank bridge,' said Pony Billy, 'perhaps it might be a tree that had been washed down by the flood?' 'Why did you not come back the same way?' 'It was gone,' said Paddy Pig, swaying himself about. 'What did you do in the wood?' 'I tumbled down. Things pulled my tail and pinched me, and peeped at me round trees,' said Paddy Pig, shuddering. 'What sort of things?' 'Green things with red noses. Oh, oh, oh!' he squealed, 'there is a red nose looking at me out of the teapot! Take me away, Pony Billy! I'm going to be sick!' 'He is very unwell,' said Jenny Ferret, 'he should be put to bed at once.' But where? In an ordinary way, Paddy Pig and Sandy slept in dry straw underneath the caravan. But everybody knows that it is unsafe to allow a delirious pig to sleep on the cold ground. 'Do you think we could squeeze him through the door into the caravan, if I pulled and you pushed?' said Sandy. Jenny Ferret shook her head, 'He is too big. We might have crammed him into the go-cart; but it is not here; it was left behind, by the ford.' 'He must sleep indoors somehow,' said Sandy. 'Why all this discussion?' said Charles the cock. 'Let our honored visitor, Mr. Patrick Pig, sleep in the middle stall of the stable. It is empty. Maggret, our mare, stands in the stall next to the window.

And there is hay, as well as straw. I, myself, scratched it out of the hay-rack. Cock-a-doodle doo! And there is even a horse rug. A large buff, moth-eaten blanket, bound with red braid,' said Charles, swelling with importance. 'The very thing! provided Maggret has no objection,' said Sandy. 'Come, Paddy Pig.' The invalid rose stiffly to his feet. But he flopped down again, nearly into the fire (which would have caused another red nose for certain, had he fallen into it). It was necessary to borrow a wheelbarrow; also the stable lantern, as by this time it was dark. Fortunately, Farmer Hodgson had bedded up the mare, and fed all for the night. He was having his own supper, quite unconscious that his stable had been requisitioned as a hospital for sick pigs. He supped in the kitchen; and the windows looked another way. Mrs. Hodgson had occasion to go to the pantry for cheese and a pasty. She glanced through the small diamond panes towards the orchard and the warm glow that was Jenny Ferret's stick fire, ' 'Tis a red rising moon. Will it freeze?' 'Bad for the lambs if so be,' said Farmer Hodgson, cutting the apple pasty. Paddy Pig did not improve; he became worse. His mind wandered. He talked continually about red noses; and he thought that there were green caterpillars in the manger. He was so obsessed with red-nosed peepers that he would have bolted out of the stable if his legs had been strong enough. 'Someone must sit up with him,'

The Effect of Toadstool Tartlets

said Jenny Ferret, 'I am no use; I'm only an old body. And you, Sandy, ought to remain on guard at the camp. What is to be done?' 'I should esteem it a privilege to be permitted to act as nurse; I am accustomed to night watching,' said Cheesebox, the smithy cat. She had arrived with Mettle, hoping for a circus show; but the company were so anxious about Paddy Pig that they felt unable to give any performance. 'I should esteem it a privilege to sit up with Mr. Patrick Pig. At the same time I should prefer to have a colleague to share the responsibility. Send for Mrs. Scales' Mary Ellen. She has an invaluable prescription for sick pigs. And she understands worm-in-tail,' said Cheesebox; 'had it been the time of the moon, we would have hung up rowan berries in the stall. But failing that propicious season, she has medicinal herbs of great virtue. Send for Mary Ellen!' Sandy looked doubtful; 'I presume she is another cat? I am afraid she might refuse to come with me, if I went to fetch her. Could *you* go, Pony Billy? Are you too tired?' Pony Billy sighed the sigh of a weary horse; 'Not tired; not at all; but my shoes are past bearing. And here is Mettle out for a lark; otherwise I would have gone to the smithy and had them altered. In any case I was intending to fetch the tilt-cart.' 'Go for the cart before your shoes are changed, Billy. You left it over near to Pringle Wood. I will undertake to have the hearth hot, long before you will reach the smithy.'

The Fairy Caravan

Pony Billy paced across the meadow in the starlight. The hill of oaks rose dark and black against the sky. On the ground beneath the trees a few lights were twinkling: whether they were glowworms or red-noses is uncertain, as Pony Billy did not go to look! On the outskirts of the wood, under an eller bush, he found the little cart where he had left it. He placed himself between the shafts and pulled – once, twice, again – what a weight! Yet the baggage had all been lifted out, as well as Xarifa and Tuppenny. Pony Billy tugged and pulled till he moved it with a sudden plunge, that took both the cart and himself over the bank into running water. Thousands of oak-apples washed out of the cart-kist, and changed into sparkling bubbles. They floated away down Wilfin Beck, dancing and glittering in the starlight. He crossed the ford, and made his way to the smithy, without any further adventure.

CHAPTER 17

Fairy Horse-shoes

The smithy was all aglow with a roaring fire on the hearth. Sparks were flying. Hot firelight flickered on the rafters overhead. It shone upon a crowd of dogs and horses,and upon the gypsies' donkey, Cuddy Simpson, who was dozing in a corner. His head drooped; he rested a strained fetlock wearily. Dogs barked; horses stamped; there was even the merry feedle tweedle of a fiddle, to which the collies, Meg, and Fly, and Glen warbled a treble chorus. And through all the din sounded the tap, tap, tap! of Mettle's little hammer on the anvil, and the creaking of the bellows that another dog was blowing. The dog was Eddy Tinker, the gypsy lurcher; and the hand-hold of the bellows was made of a polished ox-horn. 'Welcome, Pony Billy!

127

but wait for Cuddy Simpson. He has cast a foreshoe, and he is lame and weary. Wait till I fit him with fairy shoes that will make him as lish as new legs. That's why the donkeys never die! They know the road to the fairy smithy!' 'I can wait,' said Pony Billy, who was fond of Cuddy Simpson.

Creak, creak! went the bellows, keeping time to the tune of Black Nag. Louder still barked the dogs, and the horses stamped on the floor. They talked of the good old days, when roads were made for horses, 'None of this tarry asphalt like a level river of glass; none of this treacherous granite where we toil and slip and stumble, dragged backward by our loads. None of these hooting lorries that force us against the wall. Shrieking, oily, smelly monsters! and everybody has one – the butcher, the baker, the candlestick maker – even the fisherman and the farmer. Where are the patient horses? Where is butcher's Ginger? and fishcart Fanny? and baker's Tommy? Where is the hog-maned mare with the shrapnel marks? Gone, gone – all gone.

Queeny Cross, I, poor old mare, am the last nag left in a huckster's cart. But happen you like them, Mettle? you that work amongst iron and nails and bolts?'

'*I* like them?' snarled Mettle, banging the hammer on the anvil, '*I* like those snorting juggernauts? I hate them as much as you do, old Queen. They run over us dogs; they lame our cattle; they

Through all the din sounded the tap, tap, tap! of Mettle's little hammer on the anvil.

kill our sheep.' (Ragman and Roy growled low.)
'Think of the noble horses in the grand old days of
the road! Who needed a starting handle? Who
required to wind up a thoroughbred? Breed – give
me breed!' barked Mettle, 'Will-Tom's team in the
Coniston coach for me! Now it's rattle, rumble,
rattle, rattle, shriek, shriek, shriek! Gone are the
pleasant jog-trot days of peace. They have ruined
the smithies and stolen the roads. Shame upon the
Big Folks!' said Mettle, banging on the anvil, 'even
Mistress Heelis – her that was so fond of ponies –
serve her right to lose her clog!' 'Where did she
lose it, Mettle?' 'Nay, that is a mystery! It seemed
to have clog danced right away and back. It came
home by Hawkshead and it had been to Gray-
thwaite. As to the how –' (here Mettle interrupted
his story to throw a shovelful of small coal onto the
hearth) – 'as to the how she came to lose it, it was
this a-way. She had been on a long, long journey in
one of these here rattletraps; and when she got
home and unpacked her luggage, she left her clogs
upon the shelf.' 'What shelf was that, Mettle?'
'What the Big Folk that ride in motors call a
"footboard", quite appropriate for clogs. When the
car went forth next morning there sat the pair of
clogs, still upon the footboard. They looked proud.'
'One thing surprises me,' interrupted white collie
Fan, 'does Mistress Heelis really ever take her
clogs off? I thought she went to bed in them?' 'They
were off that day, sure,' said Mettle, leaning on

Fairy Horse-shoes

the bellows handle, 'I saw them pass the smithy. They grinned at me; their buckles winked. But when the car came home in the afternoon, there was only one clog on the footboard, sitting by itself. The other one had fallen off.' 'Which foot's clog was it, Mettle?' 'Her best foot that she puts foremost. She was sad. She inquired all over for her right-foot clog; and she put a notice – LOST, A CLOG – in the window of the village shop. The clog came home again after a while. My word! It had seen some fun. Now it happened this a-way,' continued Mettle, turning the donkey shoe with the tongs, and blowing white flame through the small coal, 'it happened this way. The car took the bumpy road through the woods by Eesbridge. The clogs joggled on the footboard; joggled and giggled and nudged each other with their elbows; until – bump, bump, bump! over a rise of the road, they came in sight of Joshy Campbell's tin-can-dinner-box and his big green gingham umbrella.

'Joshy was an old man with a reddish gray beard, who tidied the sides of the roads. Always took out with him his tin-can-dinner-box, and his great big bunchy umbrella. I never saw him use his umbrella; he carried it always rolled up, to keep it out of the rain. All day, while Joshy worked, the umbrella sat by the dyke, bolt upright and serious, with a long, curved, hooky nose. And snuggled up beside it sat the dumpy tin-can-dinner-box. When the clogs saw the umbrella they bounced up with

131

a shout – who-op! The left-foot clog bounced back
upon the board and continued to joy-ride; but the
right-foot clog bounced right off. It bounced onto
the road and ran back – back, back, back! back to
old Joshy Campbell's umbrella. The umbrella
made a bow and stepped out of the ditch; the
dinner-box made a bob; the clog made a gambol;
and away down the road they all ran, hoppitty hop!
without ever a stop, stoppitty stop! or the slightest
consideration for old Joshy Campbell. They ran
and they ran, and they hopped and they hopped.
For a mile or two they ran, and it was night before
they stopped.' Mettle drew the coal over the donkey
shoe with a little colrake, and plied the bellows.

'Where did they hop to, and stop at, Mettle?'
'They hopped as far as the middle of the great
wood. It was darkish; but they could see to follow
the woodland track. For a long, long way they
followed it, winding amongst the bushes; until at
length before them in the distance they saw a pool
of light. It was silvery, like moonlight; only it was
always streaming upwards; up from the ground,
not downwards from the sky above. The shining
space was level, like the floor of a great pit-stead;
it shone like a moonlit mere.

'And on that shining floor were dancers – strange
dancers they were! Hundreds of filmy glittering
dancers, dancing to silvery music; thousands of
tinkling, echoing murmurs from silver twigs and
withered leaves. And still from the dance floor a

The umbrella made a bow and stepped out of the ditch.

white light streamed, and showed the dancing shoes that danced thereon – alone.

'They tell me that in France there is a palace – a fairy palace; and in that court, long mournful and deserted, there is a Hall of Lost Footsteps, the Salle des Pas Perdus, where ghosts dance at night. But this dance amongst the oak-woods was a dance of joyous memories. If no feet were in the footgear, the shoes but danced more lightly. And what shoes were not there? Shoes of fact and fable! Queen amongst the dancers was a tiny glass slipper – footing it, footing it – in minuet and stately gavotte. She danced with a cavalier boot; a high boot with brown leather top. Step it, step it, high boot! Step it, little glass slipper! The chimes will call you at midnight; "Cinderella's carriage stops the way! Room for the Marquis, the Grand Marquis of Carabas! Make way for Puss-in-Boots!" These two danced one-and-one; but beside them danced a pair – Goody-two-shoes' little red slippers. How they did jet it, jet it, jet it in and out! And round about them danced other shoes, other shoes dancing in hundreds. Broad shoes of slashed cloth; and long-toed shoes with bells, that danced the milkmaid's morris; buckled shoes, and high-heeled shoes; jack-boots, and buskins, and shoes of Spanish leather, and pumps and satin sandals that jigged in and out together.

'And round about them – clump, clump, clump! – danced Mistress Heelis' clog, clog dancing like a

good one, with Joshy Campbell's dinner-box and
the tall green gingham umbrella!

'Only those two were different; all the other
dancers were shoes; and the main of them were
horseshoes – shoes of all the brave horses that ever
were shod, in the good old days of the road. There
were little shoes of galloways, and light shoes of
thoroughbreds, and great shoes of Clydesdales;
and the biggest were the wagoners! On they came
galloping, Ha halloo! Ha halloo! (Brill, the fox-
hound, lifted up her voice – Ha halloo, ha halloo!)
– galloping, galloping, Black Nag come galloping!
Hark to the timber wagons thundering down the
drift road!' shouted Mettle, banging on the anvil,
'hark the ringing music of the horseshoes –
here's –

"Tap, tap, tappitty! trot, trot, trod!
  Sing Dolly's little shoes, on the hard high road!
  Sing Quaker Daisey's sober pace,
  Sing high-stepping Peter, for stately grace.
  Phoebe and Blossom, sing softly and low, dear dead
      horses of long ago;
  Jerry and Snowdrop; black Jet and brown
      Tom and Cassandra, the pride of the town;
  Bobby and Billy gray, Gypsy and Nell;
  More bonny ponies than I can tell;
  Prince and Lady, Mabel and Pet;
  Rare old Diamond, and Lofty and Bet."

'Now for the wagoners! Hark to the trampling of
the wagoners!' shouted Mettle, banging on the
anvil – 'here's –

135

"Dick, Duke, Sally, and Captain true,
   Wisest of horses that ever wore shoe,
   Shaking the road from the ditch to the crown,
   When the thundering, lumbering larch comes down."

'Ah, good old days! ah, brave old horses! Sing loud, sing louder, good dogs!' barked Mettle, 'sing, Pony Billy; sing up old Queenie, thou last of the nags! Sing the right words, dogs, none of that twaddle! Now sing all together; Keep time to the bellows –

"D'ye ken John Peel with his coat so gray?
   D'ye ken John Peel at the break of day?
   D'ye ken John Peel when he's far, far away,
   With his hounds and his horn in the morning.

'Twas the sound of his horn call'd me from my bed.
   And the cry of his hounds has me oft times led;
   For Peel's view halloa would 'waken the dead,
   Or a fox from his lair in the morning."

Louder and merrier rose the hunting chorus, floating round the rafters with the eddying smoke from the forge. Till the Big Folk, that slept up above in Anvil Cottage, turned on their feather beds and dreamed that they were fox hunting.

CHAPTER 18

The Woods by Moonlight

The moon had risen by the time that Pony Billy – properly shod – trotted away from the village smithy to fetch Mary Ellen. The empty tilt-cart rattled at his heels; jumping forward into the harness like a live thing downhill; trundling gaily along the level. The pebbles on the road sparkled in the dazzling moonlight. Pony Billy blew puffs of white breath from his nostrils, and he stepped high – tap-tap-tappitty! prancing to the tune of the smithy song.

He amused himself with step-dancing over the shadows of the hedgerow trees; black shadows flung across the silver road from hedgebank to hedge. Down below in the reed beds a wild duck was quacking. A roe-deer barked far off in Gallop

Wood. White mist covered the Dub; the woods lay twinkling in the moonlight.

Up hill and down hill, Pony Billy trotted on and on; and the woods stretched mile after mile. The tall, straight tree-trunks gleamed in white ranks; trees in hundreds of thousands. Pony Billy glanced skeerily right and left. Almost he seemed to hear phantom galloping horseshoes, as his own shoes pattered on the road. Almost he seemed to see again the fairy dancers of Mettle's story by the forge.

Shadows of a shadow! Was that the shadow of a little hooded figure, flitting across a forest ride? and a dark prowling shadow that followed her? Was the trotting shadow on the road beside him the shadow of himself? Or was it the shadow of another pony? A little bay pony in a pony trap, with an old woman and a bob-tailed dog, caught in a snowstorm in the woods?

But this white road was not white with snow; and they were real overtaking footsteps that caused Pony Billy to spring forward with a start of panic. Three roe-deer cantered by. Their little black hoofs scarcely touched the ground, so lightly they bounded along. They made playful grunting noises, and dared Pony Billy to catch them; he arched his neck and trotted his best, while he 'hinnied' in answer to the deer. They bore him merry company for longer than a mile; sometimes gambolling alongside; sometimes cantering on before.

Once they saw two strange dwarfy figures.

On and on they travelled; through many miles
of woods. Past the black firs; past the sele bushes
in the swamp; past the grove of yew trees on the
crags; past the big beech trees; uphill and down.
Sometimes a rabbit darted across their path. And
once they saw two strange dwarfy figures crossing
the road in front of them – stumpy, waddling
figures, broad as they were long; running, running.
The second trundled a handbarrow; the foremost
pulled it with a rope – there go the Oakmen! Are
those pissamoor hills in the glade? or are they tiny
charcoal settings on the pit-steads? The gambolling roe-deer kick up their heels. They know the
weight of Oakman Huddikin's sledge in winter!
But this is spring. The dwarfy red-capped figures,
running like two little fat badgers, disappeared in
the moonlight behind the Great Oak.

At length the woods grew thinner. There began
to be moonlit clearings; small parrocks where the
Big Folk last summer had hung white streamers
on sticks, to scare the red stags from the potato
drills. The friendly roe-deer turned aside and left
him, leaping a roadside fence, with a flicker of
white scuts.

Pony Billy by himself reached a lonely farm-
steading; he was pleasantly warm after his long
brisk trot. He turned up a narrow yard between
manure heaps and a high stone building, that
showed a white-washed front to the moon. He
passed the doors of byres. Sleepy cows mooed

softly; their warm sweet breath smelled through the door-slats. A ring-widdie clinked, as a cow turned her head to listen to the wheels.

Pony Billy passed several more doors. Old Tiny, the sow, was snoring peacefully behind one of them. He drew the cart round the end of the shippon into a cobble-paved yard, where the wheels rumbled over the stones. He went up to the back door of the house. There was no light upstairs; the window panes twinkled in the moonlight. A faint red glow showed through the kitchen window and under the back door.

Mary Ellen, the farm cat, sat within; purring gently, and staring at the hot white ashes on the open hearth; wood ash that burns low, but never dies for years. She sat on a dun-coloured deer-skin, spread on the kitchen flags. Pots and pans, buckets, firewood, coppy stools, cumbered the floor; and a great brown cream mug was set to warm before the hearth against the morrow's churning. The half-stone weight belonging to the butter scales was on the board that covered the mug; Mary Ellen had not been sampling the cream. She sat before the hot wood ash and purred. Crickets were chirping. All else was asleep in the silent house.

Mary Ellen listened to the sounds of wheels and horseshoes, which came right up to the porch. Pony Billy's soft nose snuffled about the latch. He struck a light knock on the door with a forward swing of his forefoot. Mary Ellen arose from the

She sat before the hot wood ash and purred.

hearth. She went towards the door, and looked through a crack between the door and the door-jamb.

'Good-evening, good Pony; good-evening to you, Sir! I would bid you come in by, only the door is locked. Snecks I can lift; but the key is upstairs.' Pony Billy explained his errand through the crack.

'Dear, dearie me! poor, poor young pig!' purred Mary Ellen, 'and me shut up here, accidental-like, with the cream! Dearie, dearie me, now! to think of that! Asleep in the clothes-swill, I was, when the door got locked. Yes! indeed, I do understand pig powders and herbs and clisters and cataplasms and nutritions and triapharmacons etcy teera, etcy terra!' purred Mary Ellen, 'but pray, how am I to be got out, without the door key?' Pony Billy pawed the cobblestones with an impatient hoof.

'Let me see, good Mr. Pony, do you think that you could push away that block of wood that is set against a broken pane in the pantry window? Yes? Now I will put on my shawly shawl; so,' purred Mary Ellen, 'so! I am stout, and the hole is small. Dearie, dearie me! what a squeeze! I am afraid of broken glass. But there is nothing like trying!' purred Mary Ellen, safely outside upon the pantry window-sill. 'Now I can jump down into your cart, if you will back, under the windy pindy.' 'First rate! Are you ready, M'mam?' said Pony Billy, backing against the wall with a bump.

'Oh, dearie me! I have clean forgotten the herbs;

143

I must climb in again! Bunches and bunches of herbs!' purred Mary Ellen, pausing on the window-sill, above the cart. 'My Mistress Scales grows a plant of rue on purpose for poor sick piggy-wiggies. Herb of Grace!' purred Mary Ellen, 'what says old Gerard in the big calfskin book? "St. Anthony's fire is quenched therewith; it killeth the shingles. Twelve pennyweight of rue is a counter-poison to the poison of wolfs-bane; and mushrooms; and TOADSTOOLS; and the bite of serpents; and the sting of scorpions, and hornets, and bees, and wasps; in-so-much that if the weasel is to fight the serpent, she armeth herself by eating rue." Toad-stools! it says so in the big book! the very thing!' purred Mary Ellen, squeezing inside, and disap-pearing into the pantry. 'Bunches and bunches of herbs,' she purred, struggling out again through the broken window; 'bunches and bunches hanging from the kitchen ceiling! And a pot of goose-grease on the jam board; and a gun. And onions. And a lambing crook. And a fishing rod. And a brass meat-jack that winds up.'

'Am I to take all these things, M'mam?' inquired Pony Billy. 'Bless me no! only the herbs,' purred Mary Ellen, seating herself in the cart. But no sooner had Pony Billy turned it in the yard, preparing to start homewards, 'Oh, dearie, dearie me! I've forgot my fur-lined boots! No, not through the window this time. I keep my wardrobe in the stick-house. And I would like an armful of brackens in the cartkist, to keep my footsies warm, please Mr. Pony Billy.' 'We shall get away sometime!' thought Pony William.

Once set off, Mary Ellen sat quietly enough; never moving anything excepting her head, which she turned sharply from side to side, at the slightest rustle in the woods, hoping to see rabbits. The roe-deer did not show themselves again. The journey back to Codlin Croft Farm was uneventful. Mary Ellen was set down safely at the stable door. Cheesebox welcomed her effusively.

After assuring himself that Paddy Pig was still alive and kicking, Pony Billy dragged the tilt-cart into the orchard, and tipped it up beside the caravan. Himself he went up to the hay-stack for a well-earned bite of supper. Afterwards he lay down on the west side of the stack; and slept there, sheltered from the wind.

CHAPTER 19

Mary Ellen

Mary Ellen was a fat tabby cat with sore eyes, and white paws, and an unnecessarily purry manner. If people only looked at her she purred, and scrubbed her head against them. She meant well; but she drove Paddy Pig wild. 'Was it a leetle sick piggy-wiggy? was it cold then?' purred Mary Ellen, working her claws into the horseblanket and squirming it upwards. The result was that the top of the blanket got into Paddy Pig's mouth, whilst his hind feet were left bare and cold.

'Bless its little pettitoes! No, it must not kick its blanket off its beddee beddee!' 'What, what, what? I'm snuffocated! Sandy! Sandy! Take away this cat! I'm skumfished!' 'Was it a leetle fidgetty pidgetty –' 'Sandy, I say! Take away this awful cat!' screamed Paddy Pig.

At that moment Cheesebox entered the stable carrying a jug of rue tea, 'He sounds very fractious. Keep him flat, Mary Ellen.' Paddy Pig sat up violently under the blanket, 'Bring me a bucketful of pig-wash! None of your cat lap!' 'Rue tea,' purred Mary Ellen; 'my Mrs. Scales always prescribes nice rue tea in a little china cuppy cuppy, for poor sick piggy-wiggies with tummyakies.'

Paddy Pig swallowed the rue tea, under protest. He was sick immediately in spite of the expostulations of the two cats. Maggret, the mare in the next stall, blew her nose and stamped. After he had exhausted himself with kicking and squealing, Paddy Pig sank into uneasy slumber. But every time he turned over he kicked off the blanket, and there was another cat fight.

Towards midnight he grew quieter. The cats sat up all night; wide awake and watchful. There were noises of rats in the old walls of the stable; and noises of night birds without. Twice during the small hours of the morning Sandy's black nose appeared under the stable door. He listened to the patient's uneasy breathing, and then returned to his straw bed underneath the caravan.

At 2 a.m. the cats made themselves a dish of tea (proper tea, made of tea leaves). It enlivened them to endless purring conversations. They gossiped about other cats of their acquaintance. About our cat Tamsine, and her fifteenth family of kittens. And how Tamsine once was lost for a whole week, and came home very thin. And after all, she had been no further off than the next-door house, which was shut up empty, while the tenants had gone away for a week's holiday. But what had Tamsine been doing to get herself locked up in the next-door pantry, I wonder? 'Perhaps she was catching dear little mousy mousies,' purred Mary Ellen. 'She did not look as though she had eaten many. And to think that her people had heard her mewing, and had searched for her high and low, never guessing that the next-door house was locked up unoccupied!'

'And there was Maidie, too! oh, what a sad, sad accident! Caught in rabbit trap, poor love! She has limped about on only three footsies ever since.' 'That comes of rabbitting,' said Cheesebox, who was a stay-at-home cat; 'I used to know a black cat called Smutty, who caught moles alive, and brought them into the kitchen.' 'What, what, what! Will you be quiet, you horrid old cats? I want to go to sleep!'

'A sweet pussy pussy is Tamsine. Whose kitten was she?' resumed Mary Ellen, after renewed struggles with the patient and the blanket. 'Whose kitten? She was Judy's kitten, only, of course, she was not Judy's. Judy had a fat big kitten of her own in the hayloft; and one day she brought in a much younger young kitten, the smallest that ever was seen. It was so very tiny it could sit inside a glass tumbler. Goodness knows where Judy had picked it up! She carried it into the house and put it down before the fire on the hearth rug. Judy nursed it, and it grew up into Tamsine; but it was not Judy's kitten.' 'She was a fine cat, old Judy; such a splendid ratter.' 'Tamsine is a rubbish; she will not look at a rat; and she plays with mice, which is as silly as trying to educate them. Did you ever hear of Louisa Pussycat's mouse seminary?' 'No? Never! does she bury the dear little things? I always eat them.' 'I did not say "cemetery", I said "seminary". "Seminary" is the genteel word for school; Miss Louisa Pussycat is very genteel.

'One night I went to town to buy soap and candles, and I thought I might as well call at the Misses Pussycats' shop, as I was passing. On my way through the square I saw Louisa coming down the steps from the loft over the stores. She had purchases in a basket, and she was on her way homewards. We passed the time of night, and inquired after each other's kittens. Then, as I had hoped, she invited me to step in and drink a cup of tea, and inspect the latest spring fashions from Catchester. As we went along the cat-walk, she told me how she had commenced to keep a mouse seminary in addition to conducting the millinery business. She said, "It is remarkable how character can be moulded in early youth; you would scarcely credit the transformation which I achieve with my mice, Cheesebox." I inquired, "Do you use porcelain moulds or tin, Louisa?" "Character, Cheesebox; I refer to the amelioration of disposition and character; not to compote of mouse. I mould and educate their minds. I counteract bad habits by admonition, by rewards, and – a'hem – by judicious weeding out. Recalcitrant pupils whose example might prove deleterious are fried for supper by Matilda. *I* never have any trouble with dunces or drones. My pupils excel especially in application, and in exemplary perseverance. This very night I have left the whole seminary industriously occupied with the task of sorting two pounds of rice, which I have inadvertently poured into the moist sugar canister. Think of the time which it would have cost me to retrieve those grains of rice myself! But – thanks to my indefatigable mice – I am free to go out shopping; and my sister Matilda is drinking tea with friends, whilst my mouse seminary is sorting rice and sugar under the superintendence of my favourite pupil, Tillydumpling. I have also taught my mice to count beans into dozens, and to sift oatmeal into a chestnut." "Dear me, Louisa," said I, getting a word in edgeways, "are their fingers clean enough to handle groceries? I always think one can smell mice in a store cupboard?" "*My* mice, Cheesebox, *always* lick their fingers before touching food." "Really? and can you trust them with

'A little steep, three-storied house with diamond panes in the windows.'

cheese?" "We have – a'hem – a china cheese cover, which the mice are unable to raise. But for ordinary household duties – such as tidying and dusting – their assistance is invaluable. And they call me punctually at 8.30 – I should say 7.30 – I sit up late, you know, trimming bonnets."

'At this point of the conversation, we turned a corner, and came in sight of the milliner's shop; a little steep, three-storied house with diamond panes in the windows. (They call it Thimble Hall.) The house was lighted up; not only the shop, but also the parlour, which the Misses Pussycats only used on Sundays. "Dear me, Louisa, do you allow your mice to burn candles?" "A'hem – no. It is an indiscretion," said Louisa, feeling in her pocket for her latchkey. Even before the key was in the lock, we could hear patterings, squeakings, and shrill laughter. "Your pupils seem to be merry, Louisa?" "It must be that little wretch Tilly Didlem, who eats comfits in school. I will have mouse sausage for supper," said Louisa, opening the house door hurriedly. As we entered the passage, we encountered a smell of toffee; and something boiled over on the parlour fire with a flare-up. There was pitter pattering and scurrying into mouse-holes; followed by silence. We looked into the parlour; the fire had been lighted upon a weekday; and upon the fire was a frying-pan. "Toffee! Mouse toffee! Toffee with lemon in it. I'll toffee you! I will bake the whole seminary in a

pasty!" "When you catch them, Louisa. After all
– when the cat's away the mice will play!"

'I fancy that was the end of the Misses Pussycats' mouse seminary. Since then they have been
content to manage the bonnet shop.'

CHAPTER 20

Iky Shepster's Play

Paddy Pig continued to be poorly all next day; poorly and very feverish. The circus company were concerned and worried. It added to their anxiety that they should be detained so long at Codlin Croft Farm. The farm animals and poultry were becoming troublesome; Sandy was almost as tired of Charles the cock, as Paddy Pig was of Mary Ellen the cat.

'A change of air might do Paddy Pig good. It strikes me his illness is largely imagination and temper; listen how he is squealing!' said Sandy to Pony Billy. 'I do not like to take the responsibility of removing him without advice,' said the cautious pony, 'suppose it should prove to be measles?' Sandy had an inspiration, 'Could we not consult the veterinary retriever?' 'Would he come, think you? You and your friend, Eddy Tinker, bit him rather shabbily, two of you at once.' 'Perhaps he would come if *you* asked him, Pony William. If you would ask him nicely; and take my apologies with this large bone.' 'Where did you find that large bone, Alexander?' 'In the ashpit, I assure you, William, it smells.' 'It does,' said Pony Billy; 'I'm tired of trotting on the roads; but I suppose it must be done. The sooner we get away to the moors the better for all of us.'

'Jenny Ferret says Xarifa has rubbed her nose with gnawing the wires of her cage; and Tuppenny's hair is all tangled again for want of being brushed. But it is not safe to let them out, with all these strange dogs and cats; and Charles is not to be trusted for pecking. Look at the poultry crowding round the caravan! Mrs. Hodgson has been calling "chuck! chuck!" all the afternoon, but the hens won't go home to lay. And the worst of it is they are all clamouring to see the Pigmy Elephant.' 'Tell them he has caught a cold in his trunk.' 'That would be too near the truth; they must not guess that Paddy Pig is the elephant.'

Pony Billy thought for a moment. 'Say the elephant has gone to Blackpool.' 'Now that's a good idea! And if Charles asks me any more impertinent questions, I'll pull his tail feathers out.'

Pony Billy looked serious; 'Such a proceeding would be a poor return for the hospitality of Codlin

Croft. Give them some sort of a show, Sandy, while I am away. Consult Jenny Ferret.'

So Pony Billy trotted away once more; and Sandy and Jenny Ferret determined to give the best performance that could be arranged under the circumstances. Iky Shepster flew round with invitations gratis; and there was quite a 'full house' in the orchard. There were ducks, pigs, poultry, turkeys, two farm dogs, and the cat (which was a great disappointment for the mice who had counted upon coming). And there were also four calves, a cow, a pet lamb, and a number of sparrows.

'It would have meant a good bit of corn for us if they had all paid for tickets,' said Sandy, regretfully, 'but then the sparrows would not have come; and I have doubts about Charles. He would never have taken tickets for all those hens.'

Sandy was inspecting the audience through a hole in an old curtain which was hung on the line between two clothes-props. Behind the curtain was a small platform (in fact, a box wrong-side up); and behind the platform were the steps of the caravan. So the stage was conveniently situated in front of the caravan door. Iky Shepster directed the performance from the roof above.

'Are you all seated? (Pull the curtain, Sandy.) Cow! pigs, poultry! and gentlemen –' (murmurs and churtlings from Charles) 'dogs, cat, poultry, and gentlemen, I beg to explain that a concatenation of unforeseen circumstances has caused this performance to be curtailed gratis' (hear, hear, chirped the sparrows) 'because Mr. Pony William isn't here, and Mr. Patrick Pig is unwell, and the Pigmy Elephant has gone to Blackpool, wherefore –' 'Cluck, cur, cluck, cuck-cluck! when do you expect him back?' interrupted Charles. '– has gone to Blackpool for a month, wherefore the rest of us will present a dramatic sketch in six scenes accompanied by recitation. I should also say the Live Polecats and Weasels are poorly but the Fat Dormouse of Salisbury will be exhibited in a cage on account of that cat; likewise the Sultan –' 'Cluck, cur, cluck, cluck, cluck! my hens would prefer not to see the polecats.' 'You ain't going to see them. Act I, Scene I,' said Iky Shepster.

The door of the caravan opened and Jenny Ferret came down the steps on to the stage. She did always dress like an old woman, but this time she was dressed more so; she wore a white-frilled mutch cap and spectacles. She carried a plate and was followed by Sandy. Iky Shepster up above recited –

> 'Old Mother Hubbard she went to the cupboard,
> To get her poor doggie a bone,
> When she got there – the cupboard was bare,
> And so the poor doggie had none!'

Jenny Ferret looked inside an up-ended, perfectly empty biscuit canister (which was the only piece of furniture on the stage); in dumb show she condoled with Sandy, who was begging pathetically. Then they both bundled up the steps out of sight into the caravan. 'Cluck, cur, cluck, cluck, cluck! I've heard that before,' said Charles. 'Did not he act it natural?' said one farm-dog to the other. 'Not a single crumb! Fye! what bad housekeeping!' cackled the hens. 'Scene II,' said Iky Shepster.

> 'She went to the barber's to buy him a wig,
> When she came back he was dancing a jig!'

For this scene Sandy came on first by himself; he danced a lively 'pas seul', spinning round and pirouetting. Jenny Ferret came out on the steps with a wisp of gray horsehair in her hand to represent the wig; she stood in an attitude of admiration watching Sandy. Then she retired into the caravan; and after a few more twirls, Sandy fell flop upon the stage with all his legs in the air. 'What's the matter with him? is he ill?' asked the ducks. 'Cuck, cur, cluck –' began Charles. 'Scene III,' said Iky Shepster, hastily,

> 'She went to the baker's to buy him some bread,
> When she came back the poor dog was dead!'

Jenny Ferret wrung her hands over the prostrate Sandy. The cow appeared deeply shocked. 'Scene IV,' said Iky Shepster, after Jenny Ferret had gone back into the caravan, carrying the unwanted loaf wrapped in newspaper.

158

Iky Shepster's Play

'She went to the joiner's to buy him a coffin,
When she came back the poor dog was laughing!'

'Cuck, cur, cluck! I've heard the whole of this before,' said Charles.

'She went to the butcher's to buy him some tripe,
When she came back, he was smoking a pipe!'

'Cuck, cur, cluck! that, I have certainly heard,' said Charles. Sandy was becoming so angry that he could scarcely hold the pipe in his mouth, or restrain himself from jumping off the stage at Charles. 'Scene VI,' said Iky Shepster severely, to the audience, who, however; were all listening with respectful attention, excepting Charles. 'Scene VI, which *none* of you can have heard before, because I only invented it this minute (play up, Sandy!).

'She went to the grocer's to buy him some cheese,
When she came back the poor dog did sneeze!'

Sandy relieved his indignation by letting off a terrific 'K'tishoo!' 'Scene VII and last,' said Iky Shepster.

'The dame made a curtsey, the dog made a bow,
The dame said, "Your servant"; the dog said "Bow-wow!" '

'Cluck, cluck, cluck! very good, very good!' said Charles the cock; while the birds clapped their wings, and the dogs barked applause. 'Now,

Charles, get on the platform yourself and give us something.' 'Certainly, with pleasure,' said Charles. Up he flew and commenced –

> 'This is the cock that crowed in the morn,
>   That waked the priest all shaven and shorn,
>   That married the man all tattered and torn,
>   That kissed the maiden all forlorn,
>   That milked the cow with the crumpled horn,
>   That tossed the dog that worried the cat,
>   That killed the rat that ate the malt,
>   That lay in the house that Jack built.'

'Well done, Charles! A tale that was told in the city of Ur, of the Chaldees; and none the less interesting, although we *have* heard it before!'

The entertainment concluded with a few conjuring tricks performed by Iky Shepster, who was an adept at causing things to disappear. Xarifa's scissors were still missing, and the teaspoons were a short count.

Jenny Ferret was indignant; she reproached the bird continually. 'If you scold me any more I shall fly away without giving notice,' said Iky Shepster, sulkily. 'That is a loss we could put up with!' grumbled Jenny Ferret; 'it is my belief you are feathering your nest with teaspoons. And what for are you picking off red currant blossoms? You and that hen starling? Is it a wedding?'

Iky Shepster laughed and chittered and flew to the top of the chimney stack. He fluttered his wings and whistled to the setting sun, and to a very pretty speckled starling, perched on the next chimney pot. The ducks waddled home from the orchard. The hens became tired of waiting for the Pigmy Elephant and came home to roost. The camp was left in peace. There were white violets under the orchard hedge, they smelled very sweet in the evening.

'Jenny Ferret – please – please let me out! I want to brush Tuppenny's hair; I want to come out, Jenny Ferret!' said Xarifa, scrubbing her nose between the wires of her cage, and tugging at the bars with little pink hands.

'I cannot let you come out, Xarifa. The farm cat is sitting on the pig-sty roof; it sits there all day long, watching us.' 'Is that why the mice could not come?' 'Yes, it is. The sparrows said so. Four mice had come from Hill Top Farm on purpose to see the circus; and five others came from Buckle Yeat and the Currier. They are in the granary now, hiding behind a corn-bin.' Xarifa gnawed the bars with vexation. 'I did want to see those Hill Top mice again, Jenny Ferret; Cobweb and Dusty and Pippin and Smut. Is there no way of asking them to tea?' 'You would not like the cat to catch them, Xarifa.' A tear trickled down Xarifa's nose.

Jenny Ferret was a good-natured old thing. She said Xarifa and Tuppenny deserved a treat – that they did! and Sandy agreed with her. So he consulted Tappie-tourie, the speckled hen. Tappie-tourie talked to the sparrows who roost in the ivy

161

on the walls of the big barn. And the sparrows twittered through the granary window, and talked to the mice, behind the corn-bin. They told the mice that it would be quite – quite – safe, on Sandy's word of honour, to tie themselves up in a meal bag, which Sandy would carry to the caravan.

In the meantime Jenny Ferret had made preparations for a mouse party; cake, tea, bread and butter, and jam and raisins for a tea party; and comfits, and currants, lemonade, biscuits, and toasted cheese for a dance supper party to follow. She brewed the tea beforehand, because the teapot would be too heavy for the dormouse; so she covered it up with a tea-cosy. Then she unfastened Xarifa's cage and Tuppenny's hamper, and the string of the meal-bag; bolted the windows of the caravan, and came out; she locked the door on the outside, and gave the key to Sandy. Sandy had business elsewhere; and Jenny Ferret was quite content to spend the night curled up in a rug on top of the caravan steps, listening to the merriment within.

And a merry night it was! One of the mice had brought a little fiddle with him, and another had a penny whistle, and all of them were singers and dancers. They came tumbling out of the bag in a crowd, all dusty-white with meal. No wonder Sandy had found the sack rather heavy! There were four visitor mice from Hill Top Farm, and five from Buckle Yeat and the Currier; and there were no less than nine from Codlin Croft.

While they tidied and dusted themselves, Xarifa brushed Tuppenny's hair. When they were all snod and sleek, she peeped under the tea-cosy, 'The tea is brewed, we will lift the lid and ladle it out! I will use my best doll's tea service. Please, Pippin and Dusty, sing us a catch, while Tuppenny and I set the table. First we will have songs and tea, and then a dance and a supper, and then more singing and dancing, and you won't go home till morning!'

Pippin clapped his little paws, 'Oh, what fun! how good of old Jenny Ferret, to cheat the pig-sty cat!' And he and Dusty sang with shrill treble voices –

> 'Dingle, dingle, dowsie! Ding, dong, dell!
> Doggie's gone to Hawkshead, gone to buy a bell!
> Tingle, ringle, ringle! Ding, dong, bell!
> Laugh, little mousie! Pussy's in the well!'

Then Cobweb sang, 'Who put her in? Little Tommy Thin!' and Pippin repeated, 'Who put her in? Who pulled her out?' ('Who put her in?' chimed in Dusty.) 'Who pulled her out? Little Tommy Stout!' sang Smut. ('Who pulled her out?') Then all the mice sang together –

> 'What a naughty boy was that,
> For to drown our pussy cat;
> Who never did him any harm,
> And caught all the mice in Grand-da's big barn!'

163

'But Pussy did not catch quite all of us!' laughed Pippin. He started another glee –

'Dickory, dickory, dock! the mouse ran up the clock!'

(Each mouse took up the song a bar behind the last singer – Dickory, dickory, dock!) The clock struck one – (The mouse ran up the clock) Down the mouse run – (The clock struck one) Down the mouse run – dickory, dickory, dock!'

There was singing and laughing and dancing still going on in the caravan when Sandy came back in the morning.

CHAPTER 21

The Veterinary Retriever

Now while the mice were merry-making in the caravan, all sorts of things were happening in the stable. Paddy Pig continued to be feverish and restless; he kicked off the blanket as fast as the cats replaced it. 'His strength is well maintained,' said Cheesebox after a renewed struggle, 'we must keep him on a low diet.' 'What! what! what? I'm hungry,' squealed the patient; 'fetch me a bucketful of pig-wash, I say! I'm hungry!' 'Possibly he might be granted a teeny weeny bit of fish; the fisher-cart comes round from Flookborough on Wednesdays,' purred Mary Ellen. 'I won't eat it! flukes are full of pricky bones. Fetch me pig-wash and potatoes!' 'I could pick it for you if you fancied a little fish –' 'I don't want fish, I tell you. I want potatoes!' grumbled Paddy Pig. He closed his eyes and pretended to snore. 'He sleeps,' purred Mary Ellen. 'Which of us shall sit up first? We might as well take turns,' said Cheesebox, who was growing a trifle tired of Mary Ellen's purring. 'I will watch first, dear Cheesebox, while you take forty winky peepies.'

Mary Ellen composed herself beside Paddy Pig with her paws tucked under her. Paddy Pig sulked. Maggret, the mare, dozed in the stall nearest to the window. There was some reflected moonlight through the small dusty panes, but the stable was very dark.

Cheesebox jumped nimbly onto the manger, and thence into the hay-rack, wherein was some foisty hay, long undisturbed, to judge by three doubtful eggs in a forgotten hen nest. Cheesebox curled herself up in the hay. Overhead cobwebs hung from the broken plaster of the ceiling; there were cracks between the laths, and holes in the floor of the loft above.

The stable had been well appointed in old days. The tailposts of the stalls were handsomely carved, and on each were nailed the antlers of deer. The points served as pegs for hanging up the harness. But all had become neglected, broken, and dark; the corn-bin was patched with tin, and the third backmost stall was full of lumber. A slight noise amongst the lumber drew the attention of Cheesebox; a climbing, scratching noise, followed by the pattering of rat's feet over the loft above. Mary Ellen, in the stall below, stopped purring. Cheesebox listened intently. There were many pattering footsteps. More and more rats were assembling. 'There must be a committee meeting; a congress of rats,' thought Cheesebox, very wide awake. The noise and squeaking increased, until there was a sound of rapping on a box for silence. 'I move that the soapbox-chair be taken by Alder-rat Squeaker. Seconded and carried unanimously.' 'First business?' said old Chair Squeaker, in a rich suety voice. 'First business, please?' But there seemed to be neither first nor last; all the rats squeaked at once, and the Chair-rat thumped in vain upon the soapbox. 'One at a time, please! You squeak first! No, not you. Now be quiet, you other rats! I call upon Brother Chigbacon to address the assembly. Now, Brother Chigbacon, squeak up!' 'Mr. Chair-rat and Brother Rat-men, I rise from a sense of cheese – I should say duty, so to squeak. I represent the stable rats, so to squeak, what is left of us, so

to squeak, being only me and Brother Scatter-meal. Mr. Chair-rat, we are being decimated. A horrid squinting, hideous old cat named Cheesebox –' (Mary Ellen looked up at the hay-rack and grinned from ear to ear; Cheesebox's tail twitched) '– a mangy, skinny-tailed, scraggy, dirty old grimalkin, is decimating us. What is to be done, Mr. Chair-rat and Brother Rat-men? We refer ourselves to the guidance of your united wisdom and cunning!'

The loud, noisy squeaking recommenced; all the rats squeaked different advice, and old Chair Squeaker thumped upon the soapbox. At length amongst the jumble of squeaks, a resolution was put before the meeting by Ratson Nailer, a pert young rat from the village shop. He proposed that a bell be stolen and hung by a ribbon round the neck of that wicked green-eyed monster, the ugliest, greediest, slyest cat in the whole village; 'But with a bell round her neck we would always hear her coming, in spite of her velvet slippers.'

Every rat voted for this proposal except old Chair Squeaker. He was a rat of many winters, renowned for extracting cheese from every known make of rat-trap without setting off the spring. 'Why don't you vote? What's your objection, old Chair Squeaker?' inquired Ratson Nailer, pertly. 'No objection,' replied old Chair Squeaker, 'none whatever! But tell me – who is going to bell the cat?' No one answered.

Poor Paddy Pig!

The Veterinary Retriever

Cheesebox reached up, standing on her hind legs in the hay-rack; she applied her green eyes to a crack between the boards of the loft floor. Instantly there was a rush, a scurry, and the assembly of rats dispersed.

Cheesebox jumped down into the stall; her tail was thick, her fur stood on end. Mary Ellen very unwisely was still shaking with laughter. Cheesebox walked up to Mary Ellen. She boxed Mary Ellen's ears with her claws out. Mary Ellen, with a howl, jumped into the hay-rack; Cheesebox followed her. They sat in the hay, making horrible cat noises and cuffing each other, to the intense annoyance of the mare in the stall below.

As for Paddy Pig – who had really been enjoying a good sleep at last – Paddy Pig screamed with rage and yelled for Sandy.

While the uproar was at its height, the stable door opened, and Sandy came in carrying a lantern, and followed by the veterinary retriever and Pony Billy. The retriever was a large, important dog with a hurrying, professional manner, copied from his master. He came rapidly into the stall, wearing a long blue overcoat, and examined the patient through a pair of large horn spectacles. The cats glared down at him from the hay-rack.

'Put your tongue out and say R.' 'What, what, what? It's bad manners?' objected Paddy Pig. 'Put your tongue out, or I'll bite you!' 'What, what, what?'

'The patient does not appear to be amenable to treatment; but I can perceive no rash; nothing which would justify me in diagnosing measles' (dognosing, he pronounced it). 'I am inclined to dog-nose iracundia, arising from tormenta ventris, complicated by feline incompatibility. But, in order to make certain, I will proceed to feel the patient's pulse. Where is the likeliest spot to find the pulse of a pig, I wonder?' 'Try feeling his tail,' suggested Pony William. 'I have no watch,' said the retriever, 'but the thermometer will do just as well. Hold it to the lantern, Sandy, while I count.' 'It does not seem to go up,' said Sandy, much mystified. 'That settles it,' said the retriever, 'I felt sure I was not justified in dog-nosing measles. We will now proceed to administer an emetic – I mean to say an aperient. Has anybody got a medicine glass?' 'There is a drenching horn in that little wall cupboard behind the door,' said Maggret, who was watching the proceedings with much interest over the side of her stall. 'Capital!' said the retriever, 'hold the bottle please, Sandy, while I dust the horn. It's chock-full of cobwebs.' Sandy shook the bottle; 'I partly seem to know the smell,' said he. He held it beside the lantern and spelled out the label – 'Appodyldock. What may that be?'

The retriever displayed some anxiety to get the bottle away from him. 'Be careful; the remedy is extremely powerful.'

'Excuse me,' purred a cat's voice from the hay-rack overhead, 'excuse me – appodyldock is not for insides. My poor dear Granny-ma, Puss Cat Mew, had appodyldock rubbed on her back where she got burnt by a hot cinder while she was sitting in the fender. Appodyldock is poison.' 'In spite of our differing I agree with you,' said another cat's voice in the hay-rack, 'appodyldock is for outward application only.' 'Stuff and nonsense!' said the veterinary retriever, drawing the cork out of the bottle with his teeth. 'Stuff and nonsense! Here goes –' 'What! what! what! if you poison me again, I'll scream!' remonstrated the patient. 'I seem to remember the smell,' said Sandy. 'Quite likely,' said the retriever; 'since there is going to be all this fuss I may as well tell you it's castor oil that I have in the bottle.' 'What, what? Castor – ugh! ugh! ugh!' choked Paddy Pig, as they poked the drenching horn into the corner of his mouth and dosed him.

'A good, safe, old-fashioned remedy, Paddy Pig,' said Pony William. 'Now go to sleep, and you will wake up quite well in the morning. As a matter of fact, I don't think there is much wrong with you now.' 'I think one dose will cure me. But, Pony Billy, come here, I want to whisper. For goodness sake – send away those cats!' Pony Billy took the hint, and acted with tact; 'Mary Ellen, we are extremely obliged to you for your invaluable attention to the invalid. I shall be pleased to trot you home to Stott Farm, provided you can go at once,

171

before the moon sets. Cheesebox, we are equally
indebted to you for your self-sacrificing devotion.
I may tell you there are four rats quarrelling in
the granary, and one of them sounds like Ratson
Nailer.' Cheesebox jumped out of the stable window without another word.

Mary Ellen – after making sure that the veterinary retriever had left – Mary Ellen climbed down
into the stall and tucked up the patient for the last
time. 'Was it a poor leetle sick piggy then –' 'What,
what, what! Here, I say! Sandy, Sandy!' 'Lie still
then. I'm only seeking my fur-lined boots, they are
somewhere in poor piggy's beddee beddee.' 'Come,
Mary Ellen; the moon is setting. Good-night,
Paddy Pig, and pleasant dreams.'

'Now we shall have some peace! Those two are
worse than the rats,' said Maggret, lying down
heavily in her stall. Paddy Pig was already snoring.

The sun rose next day upon a glorious May
morning. Paddy Pig, a little thinner than usual,
sat by the camp fire, displaying a hearty appetite
for breakfast.

'No more toadstool tartlets for me! Give me
another plateful of porridge, Jenny Ferret!'

CHAPTER 22

Cuckoo Brow Lane

It is never quite dark during spring nights in the north. All through the twilight night Charles kept crowing. He was calling the circus company to breakfast, strike camp, and away, before the sun came up. Jenny Ferret's fire still smouldered; she heaped on sticks to boil the kettle. There was hustling, and packing up, and clucking of hens, and barking of dogs. 'Is all taken back that we borrowed?' asked Sandy, 'I am answerable to honest old Bobs. What about that meal-bagful of mice, Xarifa?' 'Please, Sandy, the Codlin Croft mice are tied up ready.' 'Why only the mice of Codlin Croft? where are the other nine?' 'Please, please, Sandy, might they ride to the top of Cuckoo Brow? Then they could run home all the way inside the fence.

They were afraid of owls. And besides, I did so want them to meet Belinda Woodmouse, we are sure to see her.' 'In short, they have remained; and they must be pulled,' said Pony Billy, good-humouredly. 'Here's a worse difficulty! Who is going to pull the tilt-cart? Paddy Pig is not fit for it,' said Jenny Ferret, hurrying up with an armful of circus trappings. 'That's all arranged,' said Pony Billy, 'come along, Cuddy Simpson!'

The gypsies' donkey walked into the orchard, on Mettle's four new shoes. 'Here come I, fit and ready to pull a dozen pigs! Good friends, I'll go with you to the hills for a summer's run on the grass. Fetch me a straw rope, Sandy; I'm too big for Paddy Pig's breast-straps.'

'Sandy! Sandy!' cried Jenny Ferret, 'the tent-pole has been forgotten, and our little bucket at the well. Bother that crowing cock! Where is Iky Shepster?' The starling laughed and whistled; but he refused to leave the chimney stack.

Paddy Pig was installed in the cart, to ride in state; he was wrapped in a shawl and treated like an invalid; but he was in the highest possible spirits. He played the fiddle, and squealed and joked. Sandy marched in front of the procession with his tail tightly curled. The cavalcade set off up the lane amidst the acclamations of the poultry and dogs.

Cuckoo Brow Lane is a bonny spot in spring, gar-landed with hawthorn and wild cherry blossom. It

Paddy Pig was installed in the cart.

skirts the lower slopes of the hill that rises behind Codlin Croft. The meadows on their left were bathed in pearly dew; the lane still lay in the shadow of dawn; the sun had not yet topped the Brow. As it rose, its beams touched the golden tops of the oak trees in Pringle Wood; and a faint smell of bluebells floated over the wall. Paddy Pig fiddled furiously, 'I'll play them "Scotch Cap"! I'll pop the weasel at them! Never again will I cross plank bridges into that abominable wood. Gee up, gee up! get along, Cuddy Simpson!' The gypsies' donkey trundled the cart through the dead leaves in the lane; steadily pulling in the wake of the caravan.

Tuppenny, Xarifa, and the visitor mice were all peeping through the muslin curtains. 'Is the wood full of fairies, Xarifa?' 'Hush, till we get across the water; then I will tell you!' 'Here, you mice, let me brush up the crumbs. I want to open all the windows.' (Jenny Ferret was so accustomed to travel that no amount of jolts upset her house-keeping.) 'I might as well take down the curtains, as we are going up to Goosey Foot.' 'Where is that, Jenny Ferret?' 'Spring cleaning,' replied Jenny Ferret briefly.

Xarifa commenced to explain about the washer-women up at the tarn; but Jenny Ferret bundled everybody out on to the caravan steps.

Tuppenny rolled off, under the surprised nose of Cuddy Simpson, who was brought to a sudden standstill, whilst Tuppenny was picked up amidst

squeaks of laughter. He was put to ride in a basket,
one of several that were slung at the back of the
caravan. Xarifa sat in the doorway; and the visitor
mice hung on anywhere, like Cinderella's footmen
behind the pumpkin coach. They set up an oppo-
sition fiddling, and joked with Paddy Pig and the
donkey. Indeed, Pippin fiddled so sweetly that
presently they all joined in concert together, and
the little birds in the trees sang to them also as
they passed along. First a robin sang –

> 'Little lad, little lad, where was't thou born?
> Far off in Lancashire under a thorn,
> Where they sup sour milk, in a ram's horn!'

Pippin did not know that tune, so he began
another –

> 'I ploughed it with a ram's horn,
>   Sing ivy, sing ivy!
> I sowed it all over with one peppercorn,
>   Sing holly go whistle and ivy!
> I got the mice to carry it to the mill
>   Sing ivy, sing ivy!'

Then he changed his tune, and the chaffinches
sang with him –

> 'I saw a little bird, coming hop, hop, hop!'

Then he played another; and Xarifa pelted him
with hempseeds –

> 'Madam will you walk, madam will you talk –
> Madam will you walk and talk with me?'

177

And then he heard a cuckoo and he played,

'Summer is icumen in!'

The music did sound pretty all the way up Cuckoo Brow Lane.

Where they crossed the beck there was a row of stepping stones, with the water tinkling merrily between them. On a stone, bobbing and curtseying, stood a fat, browny-black little bird with a broad white breast. 'Bessie Dooker! Bessie Dooker! Tell all the other little birds and beasties that there will be a circus show this evening. Bid them come to the big hawthorn tree, near the whin bushes by High Green Gate.' Bessie Dooker bobbed her head; she sped swiftly up the beck, whistling as she flew.

The lane was steep after crossing the stream; as they climbed they met the early sunbeams. The bank on their right was full of wild flowers; wood sorrel, spotted orchis, dog violets, germander speedwell, and little blue milkwort. 'See!' cried Xarifa, 'the milkwort! the milk is coming with the grass in spring; the grass is coming with the soft south wind. Listen to the lambs! they are before us in the other lane.'

Sandy had been in advance of the procession; he turned back. 'Wait a little while, Pony Billy; wait with a stone behind the wheel. The sheep are going up to the intake pastures in charge of Bobs and Matt. Let them gain a start before us at the

178

meeting of the lanes; it is slow work driving lambs. How they bleat and run back and forward! Their own mothers call, but they run to each other's mothers, and bawl and push!'

'Here under this sunny hedge I could pleasantly eat a bite and rest,' said Cuddy Simpson; 'put stones behind the wheels, and unharness the cart.'

'May we get down and play? we have been shut up so long, me and Tuppenny?' 'Yes, yes! go and play; but do not get left behind.'

Xarifa clapped her little hands, 'Oh, look at the flowers.' 'What is that peeping at us, Xarifa? with bright black eyes?' said Tuppenny, pointing to something that rustled amongst the hedge. 'It is my dearest Belinda Woodmouse! Oh, what a happy meeting!'

Belinda was a sleek brown mouse; she was larger than the house mice; and more active than Xarifa. Tuppenny turned shy, and stared at her very solemnly; but her sprightliness soon reassured him. Xarifa introduced her to Tuppenny, Pippin, Cobweb, Dusty, and Smut – 'Rufty Tufty I am unable to introduce, because she has stayed at home to rock the cradle. But here are enough of us to dance a set tonight on the short-cropped turf by the hawthorn bush.' 'More mice to pull!' laughed Pony Billy. 'Oh, oh! Mr. Pony William, you have swallowed three violets!' 'Well?' said Pony Billy, 'what then? I must eat!' 'I do not think they liked it,' said Xarifa, doubtfully, 'could you not eat young nettles, like Cuddy Simpson?'

Pony Billy rubbed his nose against his foreleg, and gave it up! He moved a little further up the lane, and went on nibbling.

'Can the flowers feel, Xarifa?' whispered Tuppenny. 'I do not know how much or how little; but surely they enjoy the sunshine. See how they are smiling, and holding up their little heads. They cannot dart about, like yonder buzzing fly, nor move along the bank, like that big yellow striped queen wasp. But I think they take pleasure in the gentle rain and sun and wind; children of spring, returning from year to year; and longer-lived than us – especially the trees. Tuppenny, you asked me about fairies. Here on this pleasant sunny bank, I can tell you better than in the shadowed woods.' 'Are they good fairies, Xarifa?' 'Yes; but all fairies are peppery. The fairy of the oak tree was spiteful for a while. Sit you round on the moss, Belinda, and Tuppenny, and visitor mice; and I will try to tell you prettily a tale that should be pretty – the tale of the Fairy in the Oak.

CHAPTER 23

The Fairy in the Oak

There is something glorious and majestic about a
fine English oak. The ancient Britons held them
sacred; and the Saxons who came after revered the
Druids' trees. William the Norman Conqueror
ordered a record of all the land. Because there
were no maps they wrote down landmarks; I
remember an oak in Hertfordshire, that had been
a landmark for Doomsday Book.

This north country oak of my story was less old
than the Doomsday Oak. It had been a fine
upstanding tree in Queen Elizabeth's reign. For
centuries it grew tall and stately, deep-rooted
amongst the rocks, by a corner above an old
highway that led to a market town.

How many travellers had passed the tree, since

that road was a forest track! Hunters, robbers, bowmen; knights on horseback riding along; pikemen, jackmen marching; country folk and drovers; merchants, peddlars with laden pack-horses.

At each change the road was mended and widened. There began to be two-wheeled carts. Then farmers' wives left off riding on pillions; the gentry drove gigs and coaches; and alas! there came the wood wagons.

Other oak trees were carried to the sea-port to make ships' timbers – old England's wooden walls – but the fairy's oak towered out of reach. No wood-feller clambered up to it.

Now our ships are built of steel, and iron horses rush along our roads; and the District Council decided to remove the rocks and corner, to widen the road for motor cars.

Surely it is cruel to cut down a very fine tree! Each dull, dead thud of the axe hurts the little green fairy that lives in its heart. The fairy in the oak had been a harmless timid spirit for many hundred years. Long ago, when the oak was a sapling, there had been wolves; and the dalesmen hunted them with hounds. The hunt swept through the forest; the frightened fairy leaped into the oak branches. She found the tree a place of refuge; therefore she loved it and made it her home. Because it had a guardian fairy, that oak grew tall and strong. And each of the finest trees in the forest had a fairy of its own as well.

The Fairy in the Oak

There were birch fairies, beech fairies, alder fairies, and fairies of the fir trees and pines; all were dressed in the leaves of their own special trees; and in spring when the trees had new leaves, each fairy got herself a new green gown.

They never went far from the trees that they loved; only on moonlight nights they came down, and they danced together on the ground. In autumn when the leaves fell off and the trees were left bare and cold, each fairy withdrew into the heart of its tree, and slept there, curled up, till spring.

Only the pine and fir fairies kept awake, and danced upon the snow, because the firs and pines do not lose their needle-like evergreen leaves; and that is why the fir trees sing in the wind on frosty winter's nights.

The oak fairy had danced with the pine fairies beneath the hunter's moon, because oak trees keep their leaves much later than birch or beech; but the last of the russet oak leaves were blown off by a November gale. She settled herself to sleep. The oak was enormous; tall and bold. It held up its head against wind and snow; and scorned the wintry weather.

But the Surveyor of the District Council has no sentiment; and no respect, either for fairies or for oaks!

The pine fairies were awake and saw what happened from their tree-tops further back in the

183

wood. The pine trees swayed, and moaned, and shivered. But the oak fairy slept through it all. There arrived the surveyor, his assistant with the chain links, two men who carried the theodolite with three legs; a woodmonger; and four members of the Council. They did much measuring with the chains; they made notes in their pocketbooks; they squinted through the theodolite at white and black sticks. Then they clambered up the rocks, and stared at the fairy's oak. The woodmonger measured it with a tape measure; he measured near the foot of the butt; he measured again six foot up; he reckoned the quarter girth; they did calculations according to Hoppus. The councillors said that the tree had an enormous butt; thirty foot run of clean timber to the first branch, with never a knot. They looked at the rocks; and did sums. Then they went away.

Nothing happened for six weeks; except a gale that blew down an ash tree. It crashed amongst the rocks. Its fairy fell out, shrieking. She ran up and down in tattered yellow leaves, till she found an empty bird-nest, and hid in it.

In January a number of men arrived; they had tools, and wheelbarrows, and carts, and a wooden hut. They were quarrymen, navvies, wood-fellers; and carters and wagoners with horses. They cleared away the underwood; they drilled and blasted the rocks. The noise of blasting was like thunder; it awoke every fairy in the wood.

Xarifa's Fairy Tale
See page 179

The Fairy in the Oak

And they felled the fairy's oak.

For three days they hacked and sawed and drove wedges; the wood was as hard as iron. Their axes broke; their saws were nipped; they lost their wedges overhead in the cuts. But day after day they laboured, and swung their heavy axes; and drove iron wedges with sledge hammer blows into the great tree's heart. Then one climbed the tree and tied a wire rope to its head; and they pulled with a wagon horse. The tree swayed and groaned, and the hawser broke. Again they wielded their axes; and the little fairy sobbed and cried with pain.

Suddenly, with a rending shriek and a roar, the oak thundered down amongst the rocks!

It lamed a horse, and it did the men a mischief.

All next day they hacked and sawed; they cut off its head and arms. They left the trunk lying overnight beside the road. The fairy stayed beside it, and caused another accident, upsetting a farmer's cart. His horse in the dusk saw a thing like a little green squirrel that scolded and wrung its hands.

Next day came the wagoners to hoist the great tree; and then again there was disaster. The three legs slipped; the chains broke twice – was it the fury of the little angry spirit that beat against the chains and snapped them?

At length the tree was loaded. They drew away the wagon with two extra pairs of horses; and the fairy, sullen and exhausted, sat huddled upon the log. They swept the top stones off the walls; they had every sort of trouble; but at last they reached the summit of the moor. Ten chain horses were unhooked; leaving one trembling thill-horse in the shafts. The brake was screwed on hard, to face the steep descent.

Down below the hill there sounded a humming, whirring sound – the noise of the sawmill. The fairy sprang from her tree, and fled away into the woods.

All winter she wandered homeless. One day she climbed into one tree; another day she climbed into another tree. She always chose an oak tree; but she could not settle to sleep. Whenever a load of sawn timber came back up the road from the sawmill, the fairy came down to the road.

She looked at it wistfully; but it was always larch, or ash, or plane; not oak.

She wandered further afield in spring time, into the meadows outside the woods. There was grass for the lambs in the meadows; on the trees young green leaves were budding – but no new green leaves for the oak fairy. Her leaf-gown was tattered and torn.

One day she sat on a tree-top, and the west wind blew over the land. It brought sounds of lambs bleating; and the cuckoo calling. And a strange new sound from the river – clear ringing blows upon oak.

The Fairy in the Oak

'Men do not fell trees in May, when the sap rises. Why does this sound stir my heart, and make my feet dance, in spite of me? Can I hear cruel hammers and saws upon oak-wood, and feel glad?' said the fairy of the oak.

She came out of the wood, and her feet danced across the meadow, through the cuckoo flowers and marsh mary-golds, to the banks of the flooded stream, where men were building a bridge. A new bridge to the farm, where none had been before; a wooden bridge with a broad span across the rushing river; and the straight brave timbers that spanned it were made of the fairy's oak!

'Is that all, Xarifa?' She had come to a stop.

'All except that she was happy again, and she made her home in the bridge. She lives there, contented and useful; and may live there for hundreds of years; because hard-grown oak lasts forever; well seasoned by trial and tears. The river sings over the pebbles; or roars in autumn flood. The bridge stands sure and trusty, where never before bridge stood. Little toddling children take that short cut to the school; and Something guards their footsteps by the bank of the flowery pool. The good farm-horses bless the bridge that spares them a weary road; and Something leads them over, and helps to lighten their load. It wears a russet-brown petticoat, and a little hodden gray cloak – and that is the end of my story of the Fairy in the Oak.'

'Very sweet, Xarifa, albeit longwinded. Now

mount the steps and away! White clouds sail across the blue heaven. The sheep and their lambs are on the fell; the plovers and curlews are calling. Tune up little fiddlers; begone!'

They harnessed up, they trailed away – over the hills and far away – on a sunny windy morning. But still in the broad green lonnin going up to the intake, I can trace my pony's fairy footsteps, and hear his eager neighing. I can hear the rattle of the tilt-cart's wheels, and the music of the Fairy Caravan.

GLOSSARY

Asterisks indicate Beatrix Potter's own explanations

Bedding chest, p. 83 Panelled chests with heavy lids were in use before chests of drawers.*

Borran, p. 80 A fox's hole under rocks.*

Bour-tree bush, p. 96 Elderberry bush.

Bridewain, p. 83 Wedding festivities and gifts.*

Cairngorm, p. 101 A Scotch crystal found in the Cairngorm mountains.*

Cams, p. 76 Slaty top stones of a wall set on edge like a comb.*

Cart-kist, p. 126 Body of cart, literally 'cart-chest'.

Chimney, p. 80 A rift or gully, up the perpendicular face of the crag.*

Colludie Stone, p. 85 A water-worn stone with a natural hole through it.*

Coppy stools, p. 141 Milking stools.

Cragged, p. 78 Fallen over a crag.*

Early numbers, p. 81 The old manner of sheep counting.*

Ellers, p. 118 Alders.

Foisty, p. 166 Damp and dusty; applied to hay.

Grassings, p. 81 Hill pastures which often retain their Scandinavian names to this day.*

Heaf, p. 74 A tract of unfenced pasture where a sheep is accustomed to graze; as the high fells are not divided by fences it is important to have heafed flocks which will not stray from their own land.*

Herb, p. 74 Vegetation; grass is a word seldom used by shepherds.*

Herdwick, p. 73 A distinct mountain-breed of sheep peculiar to the Lake District.*

Hoggie-lambies, p. 77 Lambs just weaned.

189

Hoppus, p. 184 Hoppus and measurements – old Lake Country complicated tables for reckoning the quantity of timber in trees.*

Hull, p. 95 A farm building.*

Hunting, p. 78 The Lake foot packs are supported by the sheep farmers in order to keep down the depredations of foxes amongst the lambs. The hound puppies on walk are reared on the farms, and returned to their homes when the hunting is over for the season. It frequently happens that a few hounds are benighted after a long chase. They take themselves to the nearest farm where they are hospitably received and cheerfully welcomed. Next morning they go on their way again.*

Intake, p. 178 A mountain pasture taken in or enclosed from the open fell.*

Keld, p. 81 A spring of water.*

Key-bit, p. 36 Ear-mark on sheep.

Langle, p. 73 To tie a piece of sacking from a fore leg to the opposite hind leg in order to prevent sheep from jumping walls.* [The practice is now illegal.]

Lish, p. 77 Active, supple, lively.*

Lonnin, p. 188 A lane.*

Lug, p. 41 Ear. As thin as a cat's lug – extremely thin.

Menseful, p. 83 Sensible or provident.

Middenstead, p. 96 A place for farmyard manure.*

Mowdie-warps, p. 76 Moles.

Parrocks, p. 140 Paddocks.

Peet, p. 73 Signifies partially blind (i.e. one-eyed).*

Pissamoor hills, p. 140 Ant hills.

Pit-steads, p. 140 Charcoal burner's hearth.

Plash, p. 76 Fall of rain (i.e. splash).*

Ridged, p. 81 Through countless generations the sheep have worn tracks along the hills, not unlike the lonely Roman Road along the summit of the mountain called High Street.*

Glossary

Ring-widdie, p. 141 A double ring shaped like a figure 8. One ring runs up and down an iron rod attached to the cow's stall; the other passes through the halter.

Rose comb, p. 101 A thick comb of many points.*

Rush, p. 76 A small avalanche, stones, snow or rock.*

Sele bushes, p. 140 Willows.

Shelf, p. 80 A ledge on the crag.*

Shippon, p. 141 Cowshed.

Skeerily, p. 138 Warily.

Snigging, p. 63 To snig or snigging – to drag a tree along the ground with a horse and chain.*

Snod, p. 163 Comfortable, snug.

Stirk, p. 82 Yearling bullock or heifer.

Stone-men, p. 81 The ancient inhabitants of the Lake District had sheep. A fragment of woollen material has been found in a stone barrow or burial place.*

Taed-pipes, p. 37 Water horse-tail – an undesirable plant.*

Tailed and marked, p. 80 Lambs have their owner's mark put on with tar or red paint and their tails cut when they are about two weeks old.*

Tarrie woo', p. 71 Fleeces of the hill sheep are water proofed with greasy preparation, on which is put a distinguishing Tar mark.*

Thivel, p. 28 A smooth wooden stick used for stirring a pot.*

Twinter, p. 76 A young sheep once shorn, 16 months old.*

Two-shear, p. 76 A twice shorn sheep, 28 months old.*

Uveco, p. 97 A cattle food prepared from maize corn.*

Wagoners, p. 63 Lumber-men.*

Webster, p. 83 Hand loom weavers.*

Widdershins, p. 97 Contrary way.*

Wilf, p. 63 The old name for willow. Wilfin is the plural of Wilf.*

Wood-mongers, p. 184 Merchants who buy and sell timber.*